FACE OF DANGER

VALERIE HANSEN

Steeple
Hill®

Published by Steeple Hill Books™

Special thanks and acknowledgment
to Valerie Hansen for her contribution
to the Texas Ranger Justice miniseries.

STEEPLE HILL BOOKS

Steeple
Hill ®

Recycling programs
for this product may
not exist in your area.

ISBN-13: 978-0-373-44433-5

FACE OF DANGER

You will call and the Lord will answer;
you will cry for help, and He will say, "Here I am."
—*Isaiah* 58:9

As always, many thanks to the other authors involved in this Texas Ranger series: Terri Reed, Lenora Worth, Margaret Daley, Lynette Eason and Shirlee McCoy.

And, of course, my Joe, who works hard to keep me fed and happy while I'm chained to my computer!

ONE

Texas Ranger Cade Jarvis gripped the wheel of his pickup truck, his neck and shoulder muscles knotting. He was on the most important mission of his career and nothing was going to stop him from reaching Austin. *Nothing.*

His glance darted to the rearview mirror. He'd been keeping an eye on the erratic movements of a set of headlights approaching behind him. The SUV was speeding, cutting in and out of the heavy traffic as if that driver thought he was on a racetrack instead of the highway.

Cade tensed. The guy was crowding everyone he passed and scattering them like a flock of scared chickens.

The dark SUV drew parallel with his truck and swerved toward him. Cade sounded his horn. There was no discernible reaction from the speeder.

Cade managed to avoid physical contact once, twice. Again. He muttered, "Sober up before you kill us both," and clenched his teeth.

The SUV matched him move for move while other drivers did their best to distance themselves from the obvious confrontation.

The reckless driver closed the sideways gap so abruptly, so forcefully, Cade couldn't dodge this time. The sound of rending, crushing, sliding metal against metal squealed through the cold November night.

Hitting his brakes, Cade braced for an even worse collision. He glanced over at the evidence case resting next to him on the seat and prayed instinctively, "Dear God. Don't let anything stop me from getting that to the forensic artist."

Tires sliding, truck body slewing sideways, Cade felt his front bumper clip the supporting post of a highway sign. The pickup's chassis did a 180 and ended up half on and half off the road, facing oncoming traffic, before Cade was finally able to bring it to a stop.

The high, bright headlights of an eighteen-wheeler were bearing down on him. He could hear the semi's air horn blasting, its brakes locking and tires squealing. Throwing his arms over his face, he prayed he'd live through the next few seconds.

The usually busy Texas Ranger headquarters building in Austin was quiet—except for the beating of Paige Bryant's heart and her niggling feeling that something wasn't quite right.

"Stop it. Just stop it. You're being silly," the forensic artist told herself as she leaned out of her studio and peered down the empty hallway. It looked as though everyone in that part of the office had already gone home for the night. Which was where she should be. Where she *would* be if she weren't waiting for a delivery.

She closed her office door and began to pace. It was only about seventy-five miles from Company D in

San Antonio to this main Ranger office in Austin, and easy, highway driving almost all the way. What could be keeping that Ranger? She didn't know Cade Jarvis well, but the few times they had met she'd been favorably impressed.

Paige huffed, disgusted with herself. *Impressed?* Boy, was that an understatement. If Ranger Jarvis was half as good-looking as she recalled, he'd be attractive enough to curl her toes. He stood nearly six feet tall, with dusky blond hair and mischievous eyes the color of warm mocha java. And when he smiled, the fine lines of an outdoorsman crinkled at the corners of those appealing eyes, though she doubted the man was much over thirty, if that.

She was about to give up on him and head for home when her phone rang. She snatched it up before the second ring. "Hello?"

"Ms. Bryant? This is Cade Jarvis," the slightly breathless male voice said. "I'm going to be a little late."

He was already more than a little late but something in his tone gave Paige pause and made her ask, "Are you all right?"

"Boy, news travels fast."

"I beg your pardon?" It was becoming clear to Paige that this call was not the result of a normal travel delay. "What news? What's happened?"

"I was run off the road not far from there."

Her free hand flew to her throat and her eyes widened. "Oh, no! Are you all right?"

"Fine. Actually, I'm in better shape than my truck is. It would have been a lot worse if other drivers hadn't steered around me after I spun out. As soon as the troopers finish their report, I'll hitch a ride with one of them and have him drop me at your office."

"Are you sure you're okay?"

"Yeah. Thankfully, there's no problem with the remains I'm bringing you, either. I had the skull packed in a padded evidence bag, so it wasn't damaged by the collision. I figured you'd probably make a composite copy to model the clay over, anyway, but I'd still like to get it to you in one piece."

"It is a lot easier—and more accurate—if I don't have to work with an original that starts out looking like a jigsaw puzzle." Still concerned, Paige paused. "Listen, if you tell me exactly where you are, I'll be glad to drive over and get you."

"That won't be necessary."

"I don't mind. It would give me a chance to peek at the evidence, too. I know how important it is to ID that victim ASAP."

The Ranger's chuckle struck her as sounding a bit cynical. When he spoke she was certain. "Oh, I get it. It's not *me* you're worried about, it's these bones."

"I didn't mean anything of the kind." Glad he couldn't see her blush, Paige realized she was embarrassed by how close he'd come to the truth. "I do care about my job," she insisted. "A lot. But that doesn't mean I don't care about living people, too."

"Hey, I was just teasing. No offense meant, ma'am."

Whew. "None taken. So, do you want me to come get you or do you think you'll be here fairly soon?"

"Hold on a sec."

While she waited, Paige listened to a hodgepodge of muted conversations in the background. Between the overlap of voices and the humming traffic noise, it was hard to pick out individual words, at least not well enough to tell what was being said.

"Ma'am? You still there?" Cade finally asked.

"Yes. What did you decide?"

"One of the troopers will give me a ride while they haul my truck in so the lab boys can take paint samples from the parts that were sideswiped. I should be at your office within a half hour. Do you mind waiting just a little longer?"

"Not at all. See you soon."

Hanging up, Paige busied herself tidying her office and trying to catch up on paperwork. Details like that always fell by the wayside when she was concentrating on drawing or sculpting the faces of nameless victims. Victims just like her sister.

Paige purposely tried to redirect her thoughts. There was nothing to be gained by beating herself up over past events. Amy was gone. Had been for sixteen years. The pretty three-year-old would probably never be located, alive or otherwise, and there was no way to change what had happened no matter how much Paige wished otherwise.

She pulled herself together and lifted her chin. "It wasn't my fault," she whispered into the silence. "I did my best to help her."

That was true. And now she reached out to other victims of horrendous crimes and gave them faces. Gave their families closure and a chance at justice. What she did was more than a job. It was her calling.

It was also her atonement.

* * *

Cade thanked the trooper for the lift, squared his white cowboy hat on his head and straightened his tie before heading toward the main Ranger headquarters. He smiled when he saw a slim woman in jeans and a denim jacket waiting for him next to the rear entrance.

"Ms. Bryant?"

"That's me. We have met before, you know." She extended her hand and Cade shook it. "In San Antonio."

"I do remember you. It's just kind of dark out here and I wasn't positive."

Actually, he'd recalled very little about the Rangers' only forensic artist other than her being in her mid-twenties and having long, dark hair that she'd kept tightly gathered at the nape of her neck. Add to that the plain, half glasses she'd worn for close work and the woman had been the spitting image of a stern schoolmarm in an old Western movie.

When he saw her this time he immediately changed his mind. Paige Bryant was lovely, with expressive green eyes and long, loosely swinging dark hair that rippled around her shoulders and brushed against her cheeks as she tilted her head.

"I waited out here for you because I figured you didn't have a key card for this door."

"You're right. Thanks."

"Is that the victim you told me about?" she asked, eyeing the blue, cubelike case.

"Yes." Sweeping his free arm toward the door he said, "Shall we? It's cold out here and I know you're anxious to see what I've brought you."

She slid her card through the reader next to the outer door and led the way to her office.

Cade had never visited this particular room before so he was taken aback. It looked more like a cozy artist's studio than it did a scientific laboratory. He spotted several computers at work stations and a small, boxy, black machine he didn't recognize. Beyond that, the place was arrayed in a personal, extremely artistic manner.

There were rows of framed pictures of faces on one wall, a window on another and tall filing cabinets on the third. Beside them hung a painting of an ethereal-looking child whose face seemed to drift in the mist of the artist's imagination.

Cade set the case on the nearest table and approached the painting while Paige removed her jacket. "This picture is amazing. Did you paint it?"

"Yes." She was unzipping the carrying bag as she spoke. "Tell me again what you know about this victim."

"Not a whole lot," Cade replied as he joined her. "We're pretty sure he's tied to Gregory Pike's murder. We just can't prove exactly how."

"I guessed as much when I was told to drop everything and give your case my full attention," she said with evident empathy. "We're all still in shock after what happened to Captain Pike. How's the rest of that investigation coming along? Any hits on the sketch I made from his daughter Corinna's description of her stalker?"

Cade nodded soberly. "Yes. We got him."

"Wonderful. How about the likenesses I created from my photos of the man in the coma?"

"Those helped, too. We still don't know his name, but

a witness saw the pictures and came forward with some information."

"So, what do you know?"

"He's Irish. The witness remembered his brogue."

"Good. At least that's a start."

"Yeah. A mighty slow one." Cade sighed. "Greg was special. He was more than my superior, he was my friend and mentor. I owed him plenty. Still do."

Paige donned latex gloves and carefully lifted the skull, supporting the lower jaw as she turned the relic in her hands to assess it. "I'm confused. What makes you think this death is associated with Captain Pike's? Under normal conditions it can take from six months to a year to reduce human remains to a skeletal state. This man must have died long before the captain was killed."

Cade nodded. "The Lions of Texas drug cartel is the link. It has to be. Did you know that Pike had ordered all of Company D to rendezvous at his house just before he was shot and killed?"

"Yes. Corinna told me all about it while I was making the sketch of the man who broke into her house. Did you ever figure out what her father was so eager to tell all the other Rangers?"

"We have an idea. Apparently, the Lions were afraid there was incriminating evidence in the house. They sent someone to retrieve it, and Corinna interrupted. Since she could ID him, he decided to take her out."

"Poor Corinna. Is she all right?"

"Yes. Now she is. When we finally nabbed her stalker, he told us he worked for the Lions and mentioned a drug drop site the Lions were still using. We put a Ranger undercover and staked it out, hoping to catch them in the act."

"Did you?"

"In a manner of speaking. We may have gotten something better." He pointed. "The skull you're holding was dug up on that property while we had it under surveillance. It's too big a coincidence to overlook. There has to be a connection between that murder and the drug cartel."

"Were you able to arrest anyone at the grave site?"

"Not at that time, but it worked out in the end. All we got at first was the jacket of the guy who was trying to retrieve the skull. Later, a man named Greco came after Jennifer Rodgers, the woman who owns the property on which the drop site and skull were located. Greco was killed by the Ranger we had working undercover there."

"Uh-oh. He didn't talk first?"

"No." Cade frowned and gestured at the skull. "If you can help us ID this guy, we may be able to make more progress than we have lately."

"What about the guy in the coma? Could he have been a secret informant for Captain Pike? He was found shot at the house alongside Pike's body, right?"

"Yeah. He's still in a coma so we can't question him, although we do have hope he may recover. They say he moved his fingers slightly. All we have to work with right now is his photo and the fact that he's Irish."

Cade tilted his head toward the skull she was holding so gingerly. "Which leaves that as our only other clue at present. That's why it's so important. So important that

I've been ordered to stick around until you finish the facial reconstruct—"

Without any warning, all the overhead lights blinked off.

Cade heard Paige gasp.

"Hold your horses," he said. "I'm sure it's nothing. The emergency generator should kick on in a few seconds."

"I wonder. Look outside. The lights in the parking lot are still working."

Cade's right hand instinctively went to his gun, his palm resting on the grip, his thumb unsnapping the tab that kept it in the holster. "You're right. Stay where you are. I'll go have a look around."

He heard shuffling. Then she grabbed the sleeve of his leather jacket.

"I'm going with you."

"Don't be silly."

"The silly part is how afraid I get when it's totally dark. Either you take me with you or I'll probably panic and get hysterical." She drew a noisy, shaky breath. "I mean it. I know it's stupid and irrational but I'm really, really scared."

"Okay. You can come. Grab the evidence. We're not leaving it unguarded."

He heard the slide of a zipper as she closed the carrying case. Now that his vision had adjusted more to the darkness he could see enough via the reflected exterior lights to move around safely, even in such unfamiliar territory.

"Got it," Paige said. "I'm ready."

Judging by the quaver in her tone she was truly frightened. Although such unfounded fears made no sense to him, he was willing to indulge her, particularly in view of the Rangers' desperate need for her talents. The last thing he wanted to do was alienate her.

They crossed the room, moving as one.

Cade grasped the doorknob. He had no sooner started to twist it than he heard a clicking, sliding sound. He froze. Was that a bullet being chambered in an automatic weapon?

If someone else was outside in the hallway, as he now suspected, they might very well be getting ready to shoot the first person dumb enough to stick his—or her—head out.

Cade steeled himself. He wasn't going to make it that easy.

TWO

Staying close to Cade, Paige kept out of the way of the Ranger's drawn gun. He'd tensed and stopped dead in his tracks when they'd heard the metallic sounds on the other side of the door.

It was ludicrous to assume they were in any serious danger. This was one of the safest buildings in the whole state. The sprawling complex of the Texas Department of Public Safety housed both the State Troopers and the Rangers. With all those lawmen roaming around, not to mention enough professional bureaucrats to scare the socks off anybody, no criminals would dare set foot in the place.

When the Ranger reached back and gave her a gentle push, she resisted. "You're not leaving me."

His tone was brusque and civil at the same time. It rumbled along her nerve endings and raised goose bumps on her arms. "Just stay back while I check. You're not going out there till I say it's clear."

"Yes, sir." Feeling contrite, Paige eased away from him slightly. The padded case bumped against her knees. She shoved it toward the hinged edge of the opening door for added security, thinking belatedly that maybe she should put her own body in its place. She didn't.

"Who's there?" Cade called loudly. "Identify yourself." No one answered, and he said more quietly to Paige, "Do you happen to have a flashlight? I left mine in my truck."

"Yes. I'll get it. What are we going to do?"

"*We're* not. *I* am."

As soon as he had the light in hand, he eased the door open another six inches, then a foot, then all the way. Swinging out in a half crouch, he aimed both gun and light first in one direction, then the other.

"Okay," Cade told her, straightening. "Looks like the coast is clear."

"Now what?"

"We find the main panel that controls the lights in this place and try to figure out what's wrong. Any idea where that panel might be?"

"Up front. We throw those breakers whenever we have a fire or disaster drill."

"That's what I'm looking for."

Paige pointed down the hallway toward the reception area. "Go that way. There's a fuse box in a utility closet. It's on the left, not far from the front door."

"Okay. Follow me. And stay close."

She chuckled derisively, positive that doing so was a lot better than letting herself be too serious. "*Close?* Trust me. That's *not* going to be a problem."

The farther they traveled, the more the hair on Paige's neck and arms prickled. She shivered. Listened to the echo of their soft footfalls. Suddenly, there was something else. *What was that noise?*

Tapping the Ranger on the shoulder, she saw the beam of the light he was carrying jump and realized he wasn't nearly as calm and collected as he'd wanted her to believe.

"Stop," Paige whispered. "Did you hear something funny just now?"

"I don't think so. Did you?" He played the light over the walls and floor and shined it into the distance, forward and behind. Its beam vanished into the gloom.

"I don't know. I thought so but now I'm not sure. I do have a very active imagination."

"In your line of work that's probably an asset."

She huffed softly. "It's not so hot when I'm trapped in a dark building, even if I do have one of Texas's finest to protect me. I was sure I heard something. Besides our footsteps, I mean."

They stood quietly together, listening to the silence, before Cade said, "Maybe you aren't the only one who stayed to work late and somebody else is trying to fix the problem, too. Come on."

Carrying the evidence bag behind her, Paige stuck close to Cade as they tiptoed along the hallway. Each private office door they tried to open was locked, as they should have been. Unless the prowler—assuming there was one—had individual keys, there was no way he could be hiding in any of those rooms.

"You said the controls for the overhead lighting are around here, right? Show me." Cade painted the beige-tiled floor with the narrow beam of light.

It took her only a few seconds to guide him to the gray metal box containing the electrical panel. He located the breakers and flipped them all to On.

The resulting illumination was blinding. Paige shaded her eyes with her free hand and could feel the tension flowing out of her. "Whew. That's better. Thanks."

"You're welcome. We'll need to report this incident to Captain Parker. It may have been just a blown breaker from a power surge or something, but an electrician should have a look at the whole system just the same. No use taking chances."

"If you say so."

"I do. Anything that scares you as much as this incident did should *definitely* be investigated."

"*Me?* I wasn't the only one on edge. You almost hit the ceiling when I tapped you on the shoulder."

"That's because I never did find a logical explanation for what sounded like somebody cocking an automatic weapon right outside your office."

"Now *that* I heard, too," Paige said. "So tell me. After what already happened to you on your way here, do you honestly think this electrical problem was an accident?"

She saw more worry than she was comfortable with in the Ranger's eyes when he shook his head and said, "No. I can't say I do."

Remaining on his guard, Cade escorted the artist back to her studio. He didn't know what was going on but he didn't believe in chance. The incident on the highway that had almost gotten him killed had been too convenient. So had this supposed power failure.

In his view, there was a good possibility that someone wanted to keep this victim's identity a secret. That made perfect sense, particularly if the Lions of Texas cartel really was involved.

Paige once again removed the skull and started to study it.

"The lab boys said he was a man in his thirties," Cade offered. "Do you agree?"

"Perhaps. I suppose they took dental X-rays and checked the opacity of the teeth to help decide." She was rotating the skull as she spoke. "It has large brow ridges and blunt orbital borders, plus a dandy occipital protuberance. Nasal openings and the structure of the inner ear fit, too."

"In English, please?"

Paige grinned. "Congratulations. It's a boy. An older one, like you said." Her grin widened when their glances met. "Probably of European ancestry. I'll check my conclusions when I look up the tissue depth measurements, just to be absolutely positive."

Cade didn't mind seeing that his request for plainer speaking had amused her. There was little enough laughter in the world, particularly their corner of it.

"Okay." He held up the open carrying case. "Better let me have him back for now. I've delayed you long enough. We can get down to serious business tomorrow."

"Fine with me. It is getting late. Max will be wondering what kept me."

To Cade's surprise, he felt a twinge of emotion that was too akin to envy to suit him. "Max? Are you married?"

Paige shook her head and the sparkle in her emerald eyes was so appealing, he almost stared.

"No," she said. "Max is short for Maximum, which

is what I named the biggest dog I've ever had. He's part Old English sheepdog, part fence-jumper, I think. I have to keep trimming his hair so he can see where he's going."

Cade gave a soft chuckle. "Well, I don't want to keep you, ma'am."

Paige stripped off her gloves and disposed of them while he zipped the bag closed. "You can leave that here so you don't have to tote it all over Austin with you," she said. "I have a big vault for secure storage."

"Thanks. After the strange goings-on tonight it'll be a relief to have it locked away safely." Cade patted the closed top of the bag. "Are you the only one who knows the combination to your vault?"

"Of course not. Why?"

It occurred to him that maybe he should keep the skull with him, even if it would be a real pain to guard it every second. "Sharing the combination is not good. I told you how important this clue is. We can't take any chances on losing it."

"I have never lost a shred of evidence. Not once."

"You probably aren't normally as edgy as you were tonight, either. Suppose somebody was prowling around looking for this skull? What then?"

"We never saw a soul," Paige countered.

"True. But if the Lions of Texas are as well connected as we suspect, they probably already know you've been chosen to do the facial rebuild."

She arched her brows and rolled her eyes, almost making Cade laugh out loud. "*That* doesn't take a rocket scientist. I'm the only forensic artist the Rangers have."

"My point, exactly," he said, watching her expression until he sensed that she'd begun to comprehend the importance of his warning. "They know what your job is."

"And maybe they were watching you instead of me and knew you'd just delivered that evidence. Did you think of that?"

"Unfortunately, yes, which means your safe is the most secure option." He took the carrying case to the safe. "Let's get this guy locked up and get out of here. I'll check in with the troopers before I go and have them keep an eye on this building. Especially your office."

To his chagrin, Paige began to laugh softly.

"What's so funny?"

"You are. You seem to have forgotten you're on foot. You don't have your truck anymore."

"It's around here somewhere. Probably still in the maintenance garage. It's dented and scraped but the running gear didn't look damaged. If they aren't through checking it for clues yet, I can probably borrow some decent wheels from the motor pool."

Taking her arm as soon as she locked the safe, he started to urge her toward the door. "Come on. I'll walk you out."

"Okay. Give me a minute to grab my things."

Cade stayed on alert and by her side as she secured her office. Watching Paige that closely, it was impossible to avoid noticing how attractive she was. Her jeans, plain green T-shirt and fitted denim jacket were extremely well suited to her. So was the soft, draping leather shoulder bag she carried. They also indicated that she wasn't into fancy clothing and such. His kind of down-to-earth, simple-pleasures woman, not given to prissiness.

Oh, well. He shrugged with resignation. He knew from his fellow Rangers that her assignments were usually completed quickly and efficiently, which meant his stay in Austin would be brief. Too bad he and Paige would never have a chance to really get to know each other.

That thought brought him up short. It wasn't bad, it was *good.* Not only were in-house romances frowned upon, he'd had his fill of ladies who fretted over his dangerous occupation so much that it drove them away. The nervous tendencies Paige had recently demonstrated meant she was not suited to being any part of a Ranger's personal life. Matter of fact, he was a bit surprised that she was able to cope with her daily tasks as well as she did.

Puzzled, he wondered what had formed such a forceful personality, yet had left an unreasonable fear of the dark and perhaps other vulnerabilities in her psyche? If he had some spare time, maybe he'd look into her past.

Just to satisfy his natural curiosity, of course.

Paige led the way across the well-lit parking lot with Cade at her side. "Do you think I need to take any extra precautions?" She smiled. "Except for not staying after hours in a deserted building while I wait for a tardy Ranger, I mean."

"Yeah, sorry about that."

"No problem. It's my hang-up, not yours."

"Well, it's always good to keep an eye out for the unusual," he said.

"Like what, for instance?"

"Anything out of the ordinary."

Although she nodded to indicate she understood and agreed, there were several reasons why Paige doubted she'd be able to spot danger before it was too late. For one thing, her head was usually in the clouds and her mind drifting, or so she'd been told often enough, first by her parents, when she was younger, and then by her friends and coworkers.

"Earth to Paige. Which is your car?"

"The baby blue pickup right over there. It's not necessary for you to walk me all the way. I can take care of myself from here on."

"Humor me."

Paige huffed and gave him a lopsided grin. "I'm starting to get the idea that you intend to do as you please no matter what I say."

Touching the broad brim of his cattleman's hat and, nodding politely, he drawled, "Yes, ma'am. And it will be my pleasure."

Being on the receiving end of the Ranger's overt courtesy made Paige feel decidedly shamefaced. She climbed into her truck while he held the door, then said, "Why don't you hop in and let me drive you over to the motor pool? I'm sure you must be tired."

He yawned, covering his mouth. "You could say that. It's been a long day."

"And a long last few months, I imagine. I can't believe the Rangers haven't solved the murder of one of their own yet."

"Neither can I." She saw him eyeing the passenger

side of her pickup as he asked, "Are you sure you don't mind?"

"Not at all." Paige concentrated on bestowing a gracious smile to confirm her invitation. She understood his frustration with any unsolved case, especially the one he was currently working. Even this many years after the fact, she sometimes found herself wondering about her sister's disappearance and wishing she could go back in time and do things differently.

Starting the engine as soon as Cade had joined her and slammed his door, Paige began to drive toward the garage where the State Troopers stored and processed their vehicular evidence.

A sudden thought caused her to hold out her hand. "You'd better give me your card so I'll have your cell number handy, just in case."

"In case of what?"

She chuckled wryly. "If I knew that, I could tell you now and forget using the phone."

"Very logical." Smiling, he pulled out a business card and passed it to her. "Here you go. I keep my cell as close as I keep my Colt .45, so feel free to contact me anytime, day or night."

"Thanks. See you bright and early tomorrow? I usually start around seven."

"Boy, you don't kid around, do you?"

"Nope. What I do is too important. When I have work like this waiting for me, I make sure it gets done ASAP."

"Understood." He saluted with a nod as he stepped out of the truck and paused. "Night, ma'am."

"Good night." As he closed the door, she hit the button

to roll the window down so they could continue to hear each other speaking. Beyond lay the garage where his damaged truck would be waiting. It disturbed her to think of how close they may have come to never getting together at all, let alone having the opportunity to discuss their mutual goals regarding Captain Pike's murder.

Paige leaned across the truck seat to watch his face when she added, "Take care of yourself."

"I will."

He'd tossed off the comment too blithely to suit her. "I mean it. I'll worry."

Cade grinned, making her glad she was still seated because she suddenly felt a little off balance—and more than a little charmed.

"Don't waste energy fretting about me," he said. "Everything will be fine. I got the evidence delivered and we'll be done with it in no time. I've heard you're a genius with clay."

"Thanks. I do have my moments."

He waved goodbye and so did she.

Watching him walk away, Paige was struck by a strong sense that, given what had already happened, the rest of this case was not going to be a stroll in the park.

That particular choice of words did not sit well. Her hands fisted and clenched on the steering wheel. Her heart began to beat faster. There was nothing peaceful or relaxing about a visit to a public park when those grounds might hide a waiting predator. She, of all people, knew that.

Pausing by the garage entrance to watch the attractive forensic artist drive away, Cade realized how much she had impressed him. Considering Paige's strong work ethic, it was no wonder the Texas Rangers were able to get by with only one artist. A person like her was worth a dozen who treated their tasks as nothing more than an everyday job.

He was totally dedicated to the Rangers, too. In that respect, he and Paige saw things in the same light. What else they may or may not have in common remained to be discovered.

He sighed and saw his breath cloud in the cold night air. Perhaps this evening at the motel, he'd see what background info he could turn up on Ms. Bryant. She would never have been hired in the first place if she'd had a criminal record, of course, but he was positive the young woman was hiding something. His gut told him so.

And, he added, if he could find out a few things to help him guide their daily, casual conversations, perhaps she'd open up and tell him what was really bothering her. Something was. He'd stake his badge on it.

THREE

The house Paige shared with Angela, her paying room-mate, and Max, the freeloading dog, was located in a semirural area outside Austin. The entire neighborhood had seen better days, but the place sure looked inviting when she pulled into her drive and her headlights illuminated the front of the property. Yes, the scraggly lawn needed mowing more often—or rather, the volunteer weeds did—and the green shingled roof should have been replaced years ago instead of merely patched, had she been able to afford it. Still, this old house was more like a real home than anywhere Paige had lived since she was a child of ten.

She reached for her purse, realizing belatedly that in all the confusion at the office she'd failed to pick up her laptop the way she usually did. *Rats.* Oh, well, it would be waiting for her in the morning.

Before she had time to reach the house, the porch light blinked on, the front door swung open and Max galloped out. From the look of him, he'd been into mischief very recently. His shaggy white beard and front paws not only looked wet, they were tinted pink.

"Glad you're home," Angela called from the doorway.

"That dumb dog just knocked over a whole glass of fruit punch and stepped in the puddle."

Paige couldn't help laughing. "He looks like it." She bent to ruffle the sheepdog's thick coat while pushing him away to keep him from getting punch on her. "What happened?"

"Max happened. You know him. If we're interested in anything, so is he. I was getting myself a drink and he tried to stick his big nose into the glass. I yanked it away and…"

"Aha! *You* spilled it."

"It was still his fault," the slightly built, dark-haired, young woman insisted. "He made me do it."

Paige continued to wiggle her fingers in the dog's thick coat while she murmured to him as if he were human. "She was trying to blame you but I didn't let her. No, I didn't. 'Cause you're the best dog in Texas. Yes, you are. You're a good boy, Max."

The black and white behemoth panted and wiggled happily all over in response to her loving tone. Since he lacked a tail to wag, he did the best he could with his whole rear half.

Laughing, Paige led him over to a faucet and held on to his collar while she tried, one-handed, to hose off the worst of the punch stain without getting him, or herself, too wet. Even in the shadowy light from the porch she could tell that the attempt was less than successful. Finally, still chuckling, she shut the dog in the fenced backyard for his own safety and ducked into the house without him.

Angela had finished cleaning up the spill and was

wringing out a rag over the sink. She grinned sheepishly. "I still say Max deserves the blame."

"I'll let you two share it." Paige eyed the packed suitcase in the hallway and her roommate's navy blue flight attendant's uniform. "You have another assignment tonight?"

"Yes. Austin to LAX via Dallas. I know it's my turn to cook so I left your dinner in the fridge."

"You ate? Already?"

"Let's just say I defrosted something," the perky twenty-something said. "And I only ate because you were so late. I have to leave here no later than eight-thirty so I didn't dare wait. You could have called, you know."

Angela's quizzically arched eyebrow was amusing enough that Paige made a face. "Okay, I apologize for not letting you know I was going to be delayed. I got involved and then distracted."

"By your work?"

"Of course. What did you think?"

Angela huffed. "Well, I have hopes that someday a handsome stranger will sweep you off your feet, but I guess that's expecting too much, huh?"

"A handsome *what?*"

"Stranger. What did you think I said?"

Paige was not about to admit that she'd thought Angela had said *Ranger.* She knew she was blushing as she envisioned the good-looking man she'd just left. Every facet of their conversation was still so fresh in her memory that she could have recited it verbatim. And those dark, compelling eyes of his. Wow!

Her gut-level reaction was what was most astonishing. She worked shoulder-to-shoulder with literally dozens of Texas Rangers, yet Cade Jarvis stood out for her like a glittering, polished gem among a pile of plain old rocks.

That was ridiculous. Insane. No doubt he turned on the cowboy charm for all women, so why did she keep recalling the way his quiet yet strong, vibrant voice had made the hair on her nape prickle and raised goose bumps on her arms? Or was that just another conse-quence of being caught in the dark?

Angela waved a hand in front of Paige's face. "Hello in there. Anybody home?"

"Barely," Paige replied with a sigh. "I was just think-ing about my new assignment. I have a feeling it's going to be a real challenge."

"Oh. Well, I have to go. You gonna be okay?"

"Sure. Fine. As soon as Max gets dry I'll let him in to keep me company."

"Just keep him away from the fruit punch. Believe me, it was all his fault that it got spilled."

"Right. Have a safe flight. When do you expect to be back?"

"Not before Friday, unless I get another assignment or decide to fly standby." Angela paused, frowning. "Why? You don't usually care when I come and go. What's changed?"

"Rough day at work," Paige said, raking her fingers through her long hair to comb it back and let it fall around her shoulders. "Don't worry about me. I'm just a little jumpy. The power went out in my office and you know how I hate the dark. If I hadn't had a Ranger with me at the time, I might have lost it, right then and there."

Checking her watch, Angela made a face. "A Ranger? As in too handsome for words?" She rolled her eyes. "*Now* you tell me, when I don't have time to stay and listen to the whole story."

Laughing, Paige shooed her with both hands. "Go on. Scram. I'll tell you all about it when you get back."

"Promise? All the romantic details?"

"There weren't any of those but I will tell you everything, I promise." She drew a finger across her chest for effect. "Cross my heart."

"Okay. I plan to hold you to that."

Paige was still chuckling softly and thinking of how she was going to explain her evening with Cade Jarvis when she heard Angela's car drive away.

Cade had managed to talk the Troopers into letting him liberate his battered truck. It wasn't pretty after the accident but it still beat walking. Besides, all his Ranger gear was in it and making a transfer to another vehicle would have wasted time.

Once he'd registered at the motel and been given a room, he powered up his laptop, made a short report to Benjamin Fritz, his captain, via email, then checked his messages. Outside of a few jokes and personal notes, there wasn't anything important. At least nothing that required a reply.

He rubbed his eyes and noticed a headache beginning to thump in time with his pulse. Thinking he'd just rest for a few minutes before doing more, he unbuckled his gun belt and stretched out on top of the bedspread. His mind wandered to Paige Bryant and the way she'd over-reacted to an apparently simple power outage.

"Assuming that's all there was to it," he argued with a yawn as he let his eyes drift closed. In minutes, he was asleep.

Nearly an hour later, Paige opened the kitchen door and called, "Max."

Waiting, she was puzzled to see no sign of him so she flipped on enough outside lights to brightly illuminate the entire yard. "Come on, Max. Aren't you hungry?"

The lovable mutt didn't respond. Paige frowned and stepped out onto the back stoop. The icy air made her shiver and fold her arms around herself. "Max? Max? Where are you?"

Nothing stirred. Slowly, deliberately, she descended the stairs to what was left of the sparse, backyard grass.

There was no valid reason for Paige to be fearful again, yet she was. Instinct kept insisting that something was amiss. Max had many faults, including being shy, but failing to answer her call had never been a problem. On the contrary, he was usually right there at her feet the moment she moved, as if she were his entire flock of sheep and guarding her was his only duty.

A rustling and whimpering behind the large evergreen bushes that grew along the house's foundation drew her attention. She bent down to peer underneath. "Max? Is that you? Are you stuck?"

Momentary relief at spotting the dog's white markings and hearing one sharp yelp was instantly replaced by shock, then dread, as she realized Max was being physically restrained.

The next moments passed in a haze of conflicting

thought. Shoes? Yes, she did see shoes. Men's dirty running shoes. And pant legs, ankles to knees. The rest of the shape of a large body disappeared into the thick leaves above except for one meaty fist that was grasping Max's collar and twisting it.

Full recognition seemed delayed, as if everything were moving in slow motion. Paige stiffened. Every fiber of her being was taut, every nerve singing with a silent scream of terror.

She started to straighten and ease away, barely able to make her feet move, partly because she desperately wanted to rescue Max.

A burly, bare arm thrust through the foliage. A hand clutched at her. Beefy fingers encircled her wrist and part of her forearm, holding tight. Hurting her.

Paige gulped air. Filled her lungs. Began to scream and kept wordlessly screaming, over and over, until she was so lightheaded she was afraid she might pass out.

Her assailant's grip merely constricted more.

All logical thoughts fled, leaving Paige feeling as if she were trapped in a horrifying nightmare. Only this was all too real.

At her wits' end, she began to twist and cry, "Help! Help me!"

The man who had grabbed her stepped out of the bushes and in doing so apparently freed Max, because Paige saw a flash of fur passing on her left.

At least her dear pet was safe, she thought, realizing that she was still in terrible danger.

"No. Let me go! Help!" she kept shouting.

Kicking and thrashing at the man who held her prisoner, she tried to land a blow that would be forceful enough to make him release her. All he did was laugh at those feeble efforts while Max circled, barking furiously.

The man's wicked-sounding laughter cut straight into her mind like the blade of a knife and made Paige so angry she lost normal rationality. The man who had kidnapped her sister had laughed like that. And she'd been too young, too weak, too frightened to stop him. Well, not this time.

She came alive. No longer feeling like a victim, she became the aggressor. Flailing with her free hand and both feet she managed to land a hard kick to the man's kneecap that made him grunt and stagger.

Then, bringing the heel of her hand up under the fleshy part of his nose, she heard a sickening crack. *Yes!* She'd done real damage.

He howled, cursed unintelligibly, and let go of her arm so he could cup his face with both hands.

Paige fell backward, landing so hard it knocked the wind out of her. Scrambling to her feet, she saw her usually timid dog worrying one of the man's pant legs. Because of the distraction, she realized she now had a chance to escape. *Praise the Lord!*

She whirled and started to run, leaving her attacker apparently trying to staunch blood from his broken nose and shake off the growling dog at the same time.

"Max!" Paige screeched as she neared the back door, hoping and praying he'd heed her command. "Max!"

Her hand closed over the knob. She twisted and jerked open the door, afraid to look behind her.

Was the man at her heels? Had Max come? She didn't dare wait to see.

A sob of relief caught in Paige's throat when she saw a large, furry, black-and-white form whiz by her legs and barely beat her through the doorway.

Slamming the door, she locked it, then leaned against it to catch her breath. They'd made it! They were safe, at least for the time being.

Now what? How do I protect us if he recovers and tries to break in? she asked herself, knowing the answer immediately. If ever there was something important to report, this was it.

She raced to her purse, found the card Cade Jarvis had given her, punched in his private cell number with shaky fingers, then plopped into the closest chair.

By the time the phone had rung twice, Paige had managed to catch her breath enough that she was positive she'd be able to deliver a clear report.

The instant she heard the Ranger sleepily say, "Jarvis here," however, she felt tears welling and a lump in her throat that refused to go away no matter how hard she swallowed.

"It's me. Paige Bryant," she managed to squeak out. "I need help. Somebody's outside my house."

"How do you know?"

"Because I saw him!" The tears finally spilled down her cheeks. "I got away but…"

"Where are you now?"

"Inside."

"Are you armed?"

"No." She heard him muttering under his breath as soon as she answered.

"Okay. Just stay put and lock your doors," Cade ordered. "What's your home address?"

She told him, then hung up and went to make sure all the doors and windows were secure. Merely knowing that the Ranger was on his way was amazingly comforting.

It belatedly occurred to her that most people would have called 911, instead. Not her. Anytime she could rely directly on the Texas Rangers for help, they'd be her first and only choice. Even the one she'd just phoned.

In her mind, that statement was immediately altered to be, *Especially* the one she'd just phoned.

FOUR

Thankful that he was still fully dressed except for his normal armament, Cade slung his gun belt around his waist, grabbed his jacket, hat and keys and hit the motel parking lot at a dead run. It only took him a second to program the truck's GPS for finding Paige's house.

Good thing he hadn't changed vehicles, he thought, his jaw clenching and hands gripping the wheel. He needed every bit of his familiar equipment, including the navigational system.

Lacking a siren or flashing lights, he nevertheless made excellent time. When he rounded the corner on to her street, he knew instantly which house had to be Paige's.

One dwelling, halfway down the block, was lit up like a Christmas tree. Not only were there floodlights in the yard, the entire house was illuminated. Every window shone brightly, as if calling to him the way a lighthouse guided mariners.

The female GPS voice said, "Approaching destination. Slow down and prepare to turn right in one hundred yards."

"Yeah, yeah, I know," Cade grumbled.

"Fifty yards. Right turn coming up."

"I'm *way* ahead of you, lady." He knew it was silly to argue with the nav unit but it gave him an outlet for his anxiety. He fisted the wheel and whipped into Paige's driveway.

There was no sign of life in the house. No human silhouettes at any of the windows.

"Good girl," Cade muttered. "Keep your head down."

He slid to a stop behind her familiar blue pickup and left his truck as he'd entered it—at a run.

Gun ready, eyes darting to any shadows that could conceal an adversary, he sprinted up the steps onto the porch and announced himself.

"It's me. Jarvis. Let me in."

His heart remained in his throat for the long seconds before Paige opened the door a crack and peeked through the narrow slit.

"It's okay. I'm here," Cade assured her. He turned his back to the doorway to face out, his pistol raised, his senses sharp. "Have you had any more trouble?"

"No. Not since I called you."

"Okay. Let's go inside and you can fill me in."

He didn't holster his gun until she'd closed and latched the door, and even then he was anything but relaxed. Noting the presence of the dog at Paige's side, he arched a brow. "Is he going to be okay with me being in here?"

Paige nodded and managed a slight smile, laying her hand atop the animal's broad head without having to bend over. "Yes. He's usually a wimp, although he did try to bite the guy who came after me out in the backyard."

"Good. I didn't understand all you said on the phone. Start over, tell me everything, and take your time." He hesitated, eyeing the windows. "After we close these drapes."

"I—I never thought of doing that. Guess I was too scared to think clearly."

"No problem. It helped me find you even before the GPS told me I was here. This place has so many lights it glows for miles."

"I told you I hated the dark."

"Fine, as long as you don't mind paying a high electric bill." He was going from window to window, jerking the curtains closed as he spoke. Her small living room contained a side table stacked with books, an easy chair and a floral upholstered sofa. There was little room for more furniture other than a television stand.

"I think the kitchen is the safest place for us to talk," Paige said as he finished covering the windows. "I did close the shutters back there. And I didn't come out till I heard you drive up."

Cade noticed the flush of her cheeks and wondered if it was from lingering fright or if she thought he had been chastising her. "You did fine. I might not have thought about drawing the curtains if I hadn't noticed how visible you'd be from the street with them open."

Following Paige and the dog, which hadn't left her side since his arrival, he was led into the kitchen. Like the living room, it looked as if it had been cut from the pages of a decorating magazine published forty or fifty years ago. The counter was made of the kind of material that was supposed to resemble butcher block. The cabinets were of the same blond color. So were the closed shutters.

He wiggled the knob of the back door out of habit and made sure it was locked. "After you called me, did you hear or see anything else?"

"No. Nothing. I think the prowler is gone."

"Probably. I didn't see anybody lurking around outside when I drove up. I'll check closer later. First, I want you to sit down and tell me exactly what happened, from the beginning, so I know what I'm looking for." He motioned to the chrome-edged dinette set and pulled out a chair for her.

Paige started to join him, then paused. "Would you like some coffee?"

"If you think it will help you focus better, fine. Otherwise, never mind."

As he watched her jerky motions at the sink he realized how close she still was to being scared out of her wits. And the enormous dog seemed to be in much the same condition. It had not left her for a second, not even to give him a quick sniff and check him out the way most dogs would have. It was as if both animal and owner were traumatized.

"Look. Forget the coffee and just come here," Cade said as he unzipped his leather bomber jacket and draped it over the back of an empty chair. He was not a patient man, especially in cases where he didn't have enough hard facts to be certain he could avert further problems.

"Okay." Paige sat and folded her hands in her lap while Cade circled to the opposite side of the small kitchen table. "Everything seemed fine when I got home. When Angela—that's my roommate—left. Max was outside in the yard."

Cade had taken out a pad and pen to jot notes as she cited the prowler's approximate age, height and weight.

It was when she began to relate the rest of her story that he leaned forward, rested his elbows on the table and closely studied her. In view of the fact that nothing disastrous had occurred, he was wondering why she hadn't regained a little more of her composure during the fifteen or twenty minutes it had taken him to reach her.

"When I called Max and he didn't come, I went outside to look for him," Paige said. "That's when I spotted a strange man in the bushes."

"And you ran."

Her green eyes misted and widened. "No! He *caught* me." Extending her left arm and resting it on the table, she displayed the beginnings of a wide band of bruising near her wrist.

Cade was astounded. No wonder she was still so upset. Without thinking, he reached out and traced the injury lightly, gently, with one finger. "I'm sorry I was so short with you. I had no idea he'd actually made contact."

To his surprise, the corners of Paige's mouth started to twitch. Was she thinking of smiling? *Now?* After all the shaking she'd been doing?

"He made contact all right," she said with a nod. "And he had a good, strong hold on me. His hands were enormous. You can see that from the marks he left."

"So, how did you get loose?" Cade glanced down to

recheck his notes. "If he was as big and strong as you say, he should have been able to easily overpower you."

The smile was now unmistakable. "I know. He shouldn't have started to laugh at me. That made me so mad I went a little crazy. *That* was what saved me."

"Really? What happened?"

"I'm not sure. All I remember is being absolutely furious and then cutting loose with more force and strength than I'd ever imagined I had. First I kicked him in the patella—the kneecap. Then, when he bent over to grab his leg, I straight-armed his face. Caught him right under the nose with an upward thrust from the heel of my hand."

"Ouch. Did you break his nose?"

"If the cracking sound was any indication, I sure did." She sobered. "I know I shouldn't be happy about inflicting pain on anyone but this guy deserved everything he got. And more."

"Did he *say* anything?"

"Nothing I care to repeat, thank you."

Cade had to chuckle. "I don't mean when you busted his nose. I mean before that. When he first grabbed you. Think. Anything? Anything at all?"

She paused and closed her eyes, her lips pressing into a thin line. Finally, she looked at him, shook her head and said, "I can't recall a thing. Not even a threat. I wish I could."

"Okay. Tomorrow we'll…" He broke off, grinning.

"What?"

Stressing the humorous aspect of his random thoughts, mostly for Paige's sake, he admitted, "I was just making plans to take you to see a sketch artist. Then, I remembered that you *are* one."

To his relief her smile returned. "That's actually how I got my start with the Rangers. I can start drawing the man I saw in the bushes right away, so I won't take any time away from work on the skull. If I hadn't left my laptop at work I could use it, too."

She pushed back her chair and got to her feet. "First I'll make us both some strong coffee, then I'll go dig out my artist's materials."

"I'll make the coffee, if you want, as soon as I get my evidence kit out of the truck. I intend to have a good look around your yard and see what I can pick up before we notify the local sheriff."

"And tell him what? That I was dumb enough to go outside and confront a prowler?"

"I wouldn't put it quite that way."

"Doesn't matter. There's more to this attack than just some lowlife hiding in my bushes." Paige was scowling. "You see it, too. I know you do. Or you wouldn't have asked me if the man made any specific threats."

It was only fair to level with her. Cade nodded as he took a few steps toward the living room. "Yes. I think it's likely that all the peculiar things that have been happening to you, and to me, are related to the Pike case. That's the most logical theory. I hope I'm wrong."

"I hope you are, too, but I'd had the same idea." She managed a smile that he could tell was partly forced. "Hurry back, okay?"

"Will do. I think you'd better follow me to the front door and lock it after me so nobody can sneak in. I won't be out there long."

The smile she'd displayed before became softer, as if muted by new tenderness. "Max and I will miss you."

"I'll only be gone for a minute or two."

The smile widened. Her eyes twinkled. "We'll still miss you." She reached for her dog and began to scratch behind its ears. "Won't we, Max?"

The kitchen table became Paige's drawing board, the Ranger hovering in the background, her catalyst. Taking information from another person and putting a suspect's face on paper or inputting data into a computer program was a lot easier when she wasn't the victim, she realized belatedly. Nothing about this sketch seemed quite right. She kept wanting to imbue the assailant's face with the evil she'd sensed rather than sticking to his basic features.

Cade handed her a fresh mug of the coffee they'd been sharing. They were already on their second pot. She glanced up at him and lifted her eyebrows. "Do you live on that stuff?"

"I've been known to, especially when I have night duty."

"Is that what this is? Are you on duty?"

"Might as well think of it that way," he said amiably. "Just because I didn't find any clues in the yard tonight doesn't mean he won't come back and try again."

"I sure hope not." She laid aside her drawing pencil. "I still don't get it. Why me? I'm harmless."

Pointing to the sketch she'd been laboring over, Cade said, "Not from where I stand. If I were a criminal, I sure wouldn't want somebody with your talent and memory for faces drawing *my* picture."

"Thanks."

The notion of someday portraying Cade's likeness struck her as a good one, although if and when she did decide to sketch him, she didn't intend to let him know what she was up to. This Ranger's portrait should be done the way she'd done Amy's, she decided. With more than just features and color. It needed feeling. The sense of strength and uprightness she felt when she was with him. She didn't intend to drape him in the Texas flag or add a superhero's cape, but that was the overall impression she intended to convey.

"So, how much longer do you plan to keep working on that sketch?" Cade asked. He was leaning nonchalantly against the kitchen counter, his boots crossed at the ankles, as he took cautious sips from his own mug.

"I don't know. Maybe all night, unless I can get it right before then. Why?"

"Because it seems sensible for at least one of us to grab some shuteye. Your couch looks pretty comfortable. Mind if I bunk there? I'm not wearing my spurs so it shouldn't hurt a thing." He held up one foot. "See?"

"Nothing except my reputation," Paige countered.

"Suit yourself. One way or another, I'm staying."

"Don't be ridiculous. There's no reason to put yourself out like that. I'll be fine."

"It's not open to discussion."

She glanced past him into the living room and shook her head. "No way."

"Why not? I'm totally trustworthy."

"I don't doubt that for a second. So am I. The trouble is, it would give the neighbors the wrong impression about me."

Cade nodded. "Understood."

"But…?" Paige arched her eyebrows. "I know you're going to keep arguing. I can see it in your face."

"Um." He began to give her a lopsided grin. "I thought I was better at hiding my motives than that."

"You're as transparent as Max is." To her chagrin, that comparison seemed to amuse the Ranger further.

"I see. Well, I guess I'm in good company then." He set his mug in the sink and picked up his jacket. "You win. I'll bunk in my truck tonight. Tomorrow, we'll discuss making other arrangements."

"Like what?"

"Like moving you closer into the city for the time being. I can get you a motel room next to mine so I'll be handy in case you need me."

"Oh, no. I'm not running away. This is my home."

"What about Max? Don't you want to protect him?"

"Sure I do. He can come to work with me." Paige could tell by the stubborn set of the Ranger's jaw that he wasn't planning to back down. He had raised some logical concerns, ones she hadn't considered before. And now that he'd started her thinking along those lines, there was also the question of how she'd know the house was secure when she returned to it after having been gone all day with Max.

She capitulated with a sigh of resignation. "Okay. I'll think about moving. Do you need to borrow a pillow or blanket or anything for tonight?"

"Nope. I carry everything I need with me in case I have to spend the night camped on the prairie." His smile returned. "Or the wilds of a pretty artist's driveway."

He'd bid her a quick good-night and was gone before she had time to react to his characterization of her as being pretty. Wondering if he'd slipped or had delivered the compliment on purpose, Paige locked the door, then stood at one side of the front window, pulled the drapes aside a smidgen and peeked through that slit until she was certain he was settled.

She'd never admit it, especially not to the Ranger, but she was very glad he'd stuck around. There was something amazingly comforting about knowing that one of Texas's finest was personally looking after her.

Returning to the sketch, she sat there and stared at it till her eyes refused to focus. Her eyelids were heavy but she refused to surrender to sleep. There was too much to think about, too many unanswered questions.

Whoever had attacked her had left them with no tangible clues. Neither did whoever had run Cade off the road and had probably followed him all the way to her office.

Between her and the Ranger, however, she was certain they'd be able to outwit whatever adversaries they might have. Their only real problem was going to be getting the skull copied in resin and the face reconstructed before something happened to disrupt the process. As long as the original skull stayed locked in her safe when she wasn't working, and Cade continued to act as her bodyguard, everything should turn out fine.

Another concern was making sure Angela didn't come home unexpectedly and get sucked into the same touchy situation.

"That's easily remedied," she muttered. "But what should I do about Cade Jarvis?" Paige could still recall his parting words so clearly it was as if he were standing beside her.

"Keep your cell close at hand and be sure I'm on speed dial," he'd said. "Any little noise, any sign that Max is upset, call me."

Even now, hours later, Paige was continuing to draw strength from him. The man's persona had seemed to fill her home completely. Overwhelmingly. Unmistakably.

It wasn't just because of his badge or the gun holstered on his right hip, either. It was much more. He was a Texas Ranger. The best of the best. Someone she not only admired, but trusted implicitly.

Like it or not, Paige knew she'd rather place her future in the hands of a man like Cade Jarvis than trust it to anyone else.

FIVE

It was sunrise before Cade awoke and pushed his hat off his face to greet the day. There was a kink in his neck and one shoulder was stiff, which was not surprising since he'd slept slouched on the seat of his truck instead of unrolling his sleeping bag in the truck's bed. The way he'd had it figured, if he stayed sitting he'd be able to race back to Paige faster, just as he had the evening before when he'd left the motel on the run.

Thankfully, she hadn't felt the need to phone again. That was a good sign, considering the very real threat she'd experienced the night before.

He checked his watch, then stretched and wiped condensation off the inside of his truck windows so he could scan the quiet neighborhood. Should he knock on Paige's door and take a chance on waking her? *Why not?* If she hoped to be at work by seven, as she'd said, she'd have to rise and shine pretty soon anyway. Besides, he wanted another chance to check her yard, in the daylight, and see if he could find any drops from the bloody nose she thought she'd given her attacker.

Cade left his hat on the seat of his truck, grabbed his evidence and shaving kits and started for the house.

His hand was raised in preparation to knock when Paige opened the door with a smile and a cheery, "Good morning."

She was wearing a pink sweater this time, and hoop earrings that he hadn't noticed before, but the rest of her outfit looked pretty much the same.

Cade grinned. "Morning. Can I come in and freshen up?"

"Sure. There's still a little coffee left over from last night, too, if you want a cup."

He made a face. "Ugh. You're kidding, right?"

"Yes." Paige stepped back and gestured with a sweep of her arm. "Come on in. I usually grab a quick breakfast on my way to work but since I knew you were going to be here this morning, I made fresh coffee."

"Mmm, I can smell it." His eyelids partly closed as he took a deep breath. "Can't start my day without java."

"I wondered if either of us would be able to sleep after all we drank last night. At least it wasn't true cowboy coffee. The stuff the Rangers brew in the break room at work is strong enough to dissolve a spoon."

"You know I'm not fussy," Cade said. He bent to offer a pat of greeting to the dog at her side. "How's Max this morning? Better?" His friendly tone and gesture were received with a wiggle and a lick at his outstretched fingers. When Paige's eyes widened in apparent disbelief, Cade asked, "What's the matter?"

"Nothing, I guess. I'm just not used to seeing Max warm up to strangers that way, especially not men wearing badges and carrying weapons. I think he has dogcatcher issues left over from his murky past—among other problems."

"Ah, I see. Well, he's clearly aware that Rangers are the good guys so it looks like that won't be a problem for me. I'm glad. It would be harder to babysit you if he didn't like having me around."

"I beg your pardon?"

Cade felt his cheeks flushing and wished he'd brought his hat inside so he could have masked some of his embarrassment under the wide brim. "I didn't mean that the way it sounded." He changed the subject. "So, point me in the right direction and I'll get cleaned up as well as I can. I really do need that cup of coffee ASAP, please. Maybe two."

"Maybe three," Paige said with a wry smile. "A good dose of caffeine might help keep you from putting your foot in your mouth again."

Laughing and smiling, he agreed. "I sure hope so. I hate the taste of boot leather and I can't afford to alienate the only forensic artist we have." Pausing, he sobered. "I will have to stick real close to you for a while, like I said. You do realize that, don't you?"

"Yes." Paige laid her hand on the crown of Max's head without having to bend over. "And while you're at it, I expect you to look after my dog, too. We're a package deal."

"That suits me. He'll be helpful in spotting anything out of the ordinary. At least I hope he will. If he's as friendly to everyone as he is to me, it may not help much."

"He won't be," Paige assured him. "He's pretty discerning, especially in regard to folks I don't like."

That made Cade's smile widen appreciably and he

arched his brows. "Really? Is it possible he's accepting me for the opposite reason? Maybe he knows you like me."

"Get real," Paige said, rolling her eyes and laughing. "I do not let my dog pick my friends."

Cade was amused by the way her cheeks grew rosier when she countered his suggestion. She might have a theoretical wall built around herself as thick as the real one at the Alamo, but that didn't mean he hadn't started to chip away at it. Truth be told, he liked Paige Bryant. It was not going to be a chore to spend time with her. On the contrary, he was looking forward to getting to know her better.

After coffee. Lots of coffee, he added to himself. Dealing with a woman as quick-witted as she was, it paid to be at the top of his game every minute.

Cade clenched his teeth as he took that conclusion one step further. Facing unidentified danger and coming out on top required the same intense vigilance. He just hoped Paige realized that.

Paige had called Angela's cell and left a message advising her not to come back to the house unless she or the Rangers okayed it first. Then she'd packed a small overnight bag while Cade was outside collecting possible evidence.

She looked up expectantly when he returned to the kitchen. "Find anything?"

"Nope. Sorry. I guess the guy made a run for it before he dripped on the ground. I checked the street, too."

"Bummer. I should have hit him harder."

"Maybe so."

Enjoying the Ranger's grin and quiet chuckle at her

candid comment, she busied herself gathering Max's leash and his water and food dishes while Cade finished off another mug of coffee.

The big dog quickly recognized the preparations for travel and got so excited, Paige had to scold him to stop him from racing madly through the house.

"You ready?" Cade rinsed out his mug and set it on the sink. "I think Max is."

"No kidding." She took a last, long look, then sighed. "I threw some extra clothes into a suitcase in the event I don't get to come back here for a few days."

"That's smart."

Paige nodded. "I suppose this kind of upheaval is normal for you but it's terribly upsetting to me."

"I do have to be ready to travel anywhere in the state at a moment's notice," Cade said. "That doesn't mean I don't like going home, though."

Paige joined him on the porch, set her small suitcase at her feet while she stopped to double lock the door. "Where is your home?"

"I've got a few acres outside San Antonio. Run about a hundred head of whiteface and keep a string of good cutting horses."

"That takes more than a few acres."

"Okay. Maybe there are more than that. I just didn't want you to think I was bragging. By Texas standards it's a mighty small spread."

"I understand." She kept her small overnight bag in hand despite Cade's offer to carry it for her, then descended the porch stairs and headed for the driveway.

"What do you do when you have to be away for

extended periods of time?" Paige asked. "Do you have help? Other supervision of the place?"

"Yes."

Cade began to grin and look at her as if he'd just heard a good joke, making Paige frown. "What's so funny?"

"Nothing. I was just thinking. If you want to know if I'm married, why not come right out and ask? I asked you. Remember?"

"What? Don't be silly. That wasn't what I meant at all."

"Okay. Have it your way." He stowed his evidence kit and the dog's things in the back of his truck with his other gear, then said, "Let's get going."

Eyeing the scraped, dented passenger side of his pickup, she backed away, hands raised, palms out. "Uh-uh. I'm not even sure that door *opens* since your accident, let alone closes properly. Thanks, but no thanks. I'd rather drive myself."

"Don't be silly. I can protect you better if we stick to one vehicle."

"And then what? Suppose I want to go somewhere later? Or suppose you get called away and strand me at work?" She faced him, hands on her hips. "I need my truck. I'm driving. And Max is riding shotgun like he always does. If you want to keep an eye on us, then I suggest you follow. That should be easy enough for a man with your fancy surveillance training."

The consternation in his expression was so plain it almost made Paige chuckle. She chose to stifle the urge rather than have him think she was laughing at him, which would have been embarrassingly close to the truth.

Their standoff lasted mere seconds. Setting his jaw, Cade circled his pickup and slid behind the wheel.

Paige was almost to her truck when he honked to get her attention. She whirled, saw him lean out the window, grinning, and heard him shout, "*No.* I'm not married."

Returning his wide smile she cupped a hand around the side of her mouth and spoke her mind without hesitation. "*That* does not surprise me one bit."

For Cade, the early morning trip back to the Austin Ranger headquarters was trying, at best. He hoped Paige's driving was normally more sensible than what she was currently demonstrating because if it wasn't, she was an accident waiting to happen. Not only had she slipped through several intersections on a yellow caution light, she'd made at least one turn without signaling first.

By the time she pulled into the lot he was ready to give her the kind of lecture usually reserved for delivery by State Troopers. It hadn't been that long since he'd worn a Trooper's uniform and he could certainly remember how to chastise a reckless driver.

When he saw the somber expression on Paige's face, however, he changed his mind. "You okay? You broke speed records getting here, you know."

"Just in a hurry to get to work. I'm almost always the first one in the building every morning. Here. Hold onto Max and my overnight bag while I find my card and keys, will you?" She passed him the looped end of the leash while she fished in the bottom of her shoulder bag. "It's a good thing I don't work in the actual forensics lab. I'd never get to bring a dog into my office if I did.

Not unless I shaved him bald, first, so his hair didn't contaminate all the evidence."

Cade huffed. "That would be an interesting sight."

"Trust me. He's really ugly under all that fur. I had to have his coat cut off when I first rescued him because he was covered with terrible mats. I'd never do it again unless I absolutely had to. He sulked for weeks."

"I can understand that," Cade said, watching her fruitless search. "What's wrong? Can't you locate your keys? You just used them to drive, didn't you?"

Paige scowled at him. "No. I keep the set for the office doors on a separate ring and the magnetic card in the same place. I'm sure I dropped them in here last night. I always use the same inside pocket."

"Since I was with you when you locked up, you might have done something different."

"I suppose I could have. I did forget to grab my laptop when you rushed me out last night. I almost always take that home with me."

She was so engrossed in her efforts to find the keys she didn't look up when Cade casually reached past her and tried the door. It opened.

He froze, instantly on alert. "Hold it. Something's wrong. This should be a secure entrance."

"You're right. Even if one of the others came in earlier, that door would still be locked. Maybe the mechanism was messed up during the power failure last night."

"You don't really believe that, do you?"

"No. I suppose I don't."

Cade set her things on the ground, handed her Max's leash, then drew his gun. "It doesn't look like it was jimmied. You wait out here till I check."

"But…"

This time he was not going to let her have her way. Not when it might mean compromising her safety. "Listen, lady. You can be as crazy-independent as you want as long as you do it on your own time. While I'm responsible for you, you'll listen to me. Got it?"

"Yes, sir."

If she had saluted to accompany her flippant-sounding reply he might have been angry. Since she didn't, he wasn't sure whether or not she was mocking him so he ignored the possibility. There were other far more pressing concerns, such as, were they simply going to Paige's studio or might they be walking into a trap?

Cade slipped through the exterior door and glanced back to be certain Paige was obeying his orders before he started down the hallway. Thankfully, she was right where he'd left her.

The first thing he noticed was tiny bits of glass glittering on the polished tile floor, as if they'd been tracked there. Following the trail of scattered glass fragments, he came to the door of Paige's studio. It was standing half-open but didn't appear to have been kicked or pried to break the latch.

He flattened against the exterior wall, gun in hand, and prepared his mind before whipping around the corner and taking dead aim at the room's interior.

Nothing moved. There was no sound except for Cade's shout of "Rangers. Show yourself."

There was no hiding place big enough to conceal a grown man in the crowded office, he reasoned, remaining on alert just the same. His training insisted that he check carefully no matter how cut and dried a situation seemed on the surface.

Cade inched his way into the room and poked into every nook and cranny. Whoever had committed this act was obviously long gone. The studio was deserted. What was left of it. He wasn't sure exactly how bad the damage would prove to be once all the broken equipment and rifled files were sorted out, but at first glance this destruction was far, far worse than he'd feared. The only positive sign was that the enormous evidence vault apparently hadn't been opened.

He thumbed the safety of the .45 into place and holstered it. The crime-lab boys would want to go over this scene in detail before Paige was allowed back in. He grimaced. He'd sooner face a room full of riled-up rattlers than have to deliver that kind of unwelcome news to her.

As Cade inched his way out through the half-open door, a further disturbing thought crossed his mind. Two doors that definitely should have been locked, were not. And Paige's office keys were missing. Unless she located them or came up with a different, plausible explanation, it was highly likely that her purse had been searched and robbed sometime last night, perhaps while she'd been fighting off her attacker in the yard.

Therefore, chances were very good that someone had been inside her house. The sooner he got her into official protective custody, the better. That was going to happen whether she liked the idea or not.

He was going to see to it.

SIX

The sight of the stalwart Ranger returning was such a relief Paige had to smile. Instead of mirroring her mood, he was scowling.

"Everything's fine, right?" she called.

Cade shook his head as he ushered her away from the door. "Far from it, I'm afraid. We'll need to have a forensics team go over your studio, inch by inch, before you can go back to work. Sorry."

"What are you talking about?" She tried to sidle past him.

"It's been ransacked," Cade explained. He held out his arm to stop her from passing. "And there's broken glass all over the floor. You can't take Max in there. His feet will be cut to ribbons."

"Then you look after him. Here." She offered the looped end of the leash to the Ranger. "I want to see for myself."

"You will. Soon. You, of all people, ought to know how important it is to keep from disturbing a crime scene."

A crime scene? Her lovely studio with all its high-tech equipment as well as her personal items? She shivered, then backed away with Max while she tried to sort out her whirling, darting thoughts.

"Okay. I suppose you're right," Paige finally said. "But I am going to go peek in the window."

"Only if there's no sign that that area was recently disturbed," Cade warned. "You know the drill."

"Yes, except it feels a lot different now that I'm the victim." She made a face. "*Again.* I suppose that's normal. You wouldn't like it if somebody ransacked your ranch."

Cade gave her a fleeting half smile and nodded. "You're right about that. I wasn't real pleased when they smashed in the side of my truck, either."

"See?"

Standing aside and stewing, Paige waited while he notified dispatch and explained their situation. Since her office was located in the same sprawling complex as the other Texas Department of Public Services branches, the response time would naturally be very short.

And then what? she asked herself. What could she do if she couldn't work with her own computers or laser scanner? There were similar systems available elsewhere, yes, but they were needed for other tasks. Plus, as far as she knew, nobody nearby had the latest version of the software she used to identify and reconstruct faces, not to mention the availability of properly stored clay and all her modeling tools.

She was still stewing over the anticipated delay when Cade took her elbow. "Okay. Help's on the way. Now come on. If you want to look in any windows we'd better do it before the first responders get here."

"Whoa." Paige twisted her arm free from his grasp. "You just watch my stuff. I'll take care of the rest."

"Uh-uh. No way, lady. I can't guard you if you're running all over the place without me." He grinned. "Besides, Max wants to go, too. Don't you old boy?"

Paige arched her eyebrows for emphasis as she groaned. It was impossible to stay mad at this stubborn man for very long no matter how hard she tried. He was funny and clever and… And she wanted him with her, although she was loathe to admit it, particularly to him.

"I give up." She passed the leash and her shoulder bag to Cade. He looked so amusing she giggled.

"What's so funny?"

"You are. You look more like a bellman than a typical, tough Texas Ranger."

He nodded while scanning the lawns, parking lots and surrounding buildings. "I just thought of that, too. I hope there's nothing breakable in any of this because if I need to draw my gun, I'm dropping it."

"Okay. Come on." Starting around the building, she kept thinking about all that had happened to her recently. "I certainly hope they find enough clues in my office to lead to an arrest. I'm getting tired of feeling like there's a big, red bull's-eye painted smack in the middle of my back."

Hesitating, she looked over her shoulder at the Ranger as he brought up the rear. "We have to figure all this out," she insisted. "I'm not only worried about my work, I don't know what I'd do if anything bad happened to Max. He's my best friend."

"Yeah. I know. And I understand. I had a favorite ranch dog when I was a kid."

As Paige turned down the east side of the building toward the only outside window of her studio, she decided to give the Ranger a little additional information. "I was never allowed to have a pet when I was little."

"Why not? Was someone in your family allergic?"

"No. Nothing like that. I…" She paused to carefully monitor her thoughts. "Mother said I wasn't responsible enough to care for a puppy."

"Couldn't you have offered to prove you were capable by giving it a try?"

"No." Paige shook her head adamantly. "By that time, my parents were convinced that I was the most unreliable person in the world." She bit her lip. "And I agreed with them."

Puzzled by her criticism, Cade hung back, frowning while Paige slowly approached the window. "I don't see any footprints in the dirt," she said. "Just the marks from where the groundskeepers have raked. It should be okay to go close enough to look in."

He couldn't argue. If it had been his territory that had been violated, he knew he'd be as adamant about surveying the damage as she was.

Watching her tiptoe up to the window, he saw her cup her hands around her face to cut the glare of the morning sun and heard a sharp intake of breath as she peered in.

Paige whirled, her eyes wide. "What a mess! Who's doing all this?"

"Probably somebody who really wants to stop us from

reconstructing the face and solving the old murder—and Greg Pike's as well, just like we thought."

"Keep reminding me, okay? Otherwise I might start to think I have a lot of enemies."

Cade heard the wail of sirens coming from several directions. "Here comes help. Will you be okay if I leave you for a little while?"

"Sure. Why not?" She looked toward the first patrol car as it entered the parking lot with its lights flashing. "I'll be surrounded by Troopers and other Rangers. Just don't be gone too long. Okay?"

"Okay."

Dropping everything onto a bench close to the main area of activity and passing her the leash, he said, "Sit right here and wait for me. I'll make this as fast as I can."

He could tell by her expression that she was distressed. Who wouldn't be? "As soon as I'm done, we'll go somewhere and grab breakfast to give the techs a chance to finish checking your office. Okay?"

"I won't know where to start to put everything back. Those vandals *trashed* the place."

"It may not be as bad as it looks," Cade offered. "And with two of us working, we'll have it back in shape in no time."

"If my computers are wrecked I'll have to get them replaced and then reload all my programs and data. That might take days."

"If it does, it does. The important thing is reconstructing the face."

She inhaled sharply. "They didn't get the safe open, did they? Tell me they didn't."

"No. They didn't. There were a few scratches around the lock but the door was shut tight so I figure they tried and failed. If you're worried, I'll have somebody open it just to be sure."

"Thank God. Literally."

Smiling, he gave her a good Southern-sounding "Amen," before adding, "I'll do whatever you say to help you get back to work ASAP. I promise."

"I believe you," Paige said. "And…Ranger…thanks."

It sounded to Cade as if she'd almost slipped and called him by his given name instead of his rank. He took that as a favorable sign.

"Tell you what, *Paige*—if you'll allow me to be that informal," he drawled, trying to ease the tension by stressing nonchalance. "I think it would be nice if we both relaxed a little and used each other's first names. I'm Cade."

"I know."

The slight smile that lifted the corners of her mouth gave him hope that she'd agree to lower her guard. He wasn't asking for a complete absence of formality, just a little more camaraderie. After all, they'd be together until this project was completed and the better they got along, the quicker they'd see results.

As Cade watched, her smile grew and there was a glint of emerald clarity in her gaze that gave him added assurance. "It's all right, then?" he asked.

"Yes," she said, "as long as you don't call me *Miss* Paige the way some of the other Rangers around here do. I know it's common practice for Texans to do that but it makes me feel like somebody's grandmother."

"Fair enough."

Another Trooper's car sped around the corner and into the nearby lot to join two that were already there. Uniformed officers were crossing the lawn and hurrying toward them.

"Here comes the cavalry," Cade said. "You sure you'll be all right?"

"We'll be fine. Just hurry back."

That went without saying, Cade thought as he turned to face the approaching hoard and prepared to explain what he'd discovered. Parting from this particular woman was getting harder and harder. It wasn't the first time he'd felt a proprietary responsibility toward a victim but it was odd to have that same feeling regarding one of the Rangers' own. Paige was his coworker, and as such she should have been off-limits to him no matter how attracted he might be to her.

The one element that struck him strongest was the sense that he had been sent to Austin specifically to look after her, as if God had been in the details. He supposed that was possible. He'd certainly prayed for a soul mate often enough, yet had never dreamed he might come across one at work.

It wasn't wrong to be dedicated to guarding her against threats, seen and unseen, Cade told himself. And it certainly was human nature to be attracted to a lovely, single, young woman who was pretty much perfect, at least as far as he could tell. The problem was that his heart and mind must always remain focused on whatever was in the best interests of the Rangers, no matter how that might affect him personally.

He sighed, half disgusted with himself, half hoping that the Lord was working all things for his good, the way the Scripture in the book of Romans promised.

"If that's the case, Father," Cade prayed in a whisper, "I'd sure like to have a sign that it's okay to let myself think about Paige the way I'm starting to, because if You're not involved in all this, I could be making a big, big mistake."

As if it was my first one, he countered, remembering the way he'd been certain that another woman he'd dated a few years back was going to make a perfect wife. Then he'd learned that she'd expected him to turn in his star and leave law enforcement to please her.

Cade's jaw clenched. There were some things a man just knew were right. His place within the Rangers was one of them. As far as he was concerned, he'd been born to become a Texas Ranger, had dreamed of it from a young age.

Yes, his job could be dangerous. That went without saying. But what he was doing was akin to a sacred duty, a task that charged him with the welfare of the citizens in his care and meant that he must always try to right any wrongs that had befallen them.

Such as the victims whose cases he was currently working as a member of UCIT, the Unsolved Crimes Investigation Team. Gregory Pike's case was at the top of his list. Not everyone had what it took to be a Texas Ranger but Greg had recognized the skills and mindset in Cade and had urged him to apply. His was a job he would never shirk. Not for any reason.

Although he extended his hand to the closest Trooper

and formally introduced himself, a part of Cade's mind remained with Paige. To his chagrin, a part of his heart did the same.

Paige watched the ongoing furor as more and more men and women arrived and either poured into the office building or gathered in small groups to share information and secure the perimeter.

The tall, graying Ranger, Doug Parker, met her gaze, excused himself from the others and approached her.

"You okay, Miss Paige?"

She nodded. "Yes, sir. I wasn't in my studio when it happened. The place was already trashed when I got here early this morning."

"Any idea what's going on?"

"The UCIT man from Company D thinks the burglars may have been after the skull he just brought me to work on."

Thoughtful, Captain Parker pushed up the front brim of his white hat with one gnarled finger. "Any idea why?"

"He did mention that he thought the Lions of Texas and Captain Pike's murder might all be connected to the face I'm about to reconstruct."

"Hmm. Possible. If you want to come to my office later, we can discuss those theories," the captain said. He looked around. "Where is the UCIT Ranger, anyway?"

"Over there. Just coming out of our building," Paige said, pointing.

"Jarvis. A good man." Parker was nodding thoughtfully and squinting at Cade. "I am a little surprised he opened up to you so much, though."

"He said he felt it was important for me to know enough details pertaining to the case to be on my guard."

"Why would he think you'd need to do that? You didn't know about this burglary then, did you?"

"No. But last night, at home, I stumbled on a prowler in my yard. I barely escaped." She pushed back the cuff of her jacket to display part of the purplish bruise that now extended halfway to her elbow as well as circling her wrist.

Parker's eyes widened in surprise. "Have you seen a doctor?"

"I don't think that's necessary. The guy who grabbed me probably needed one, though. I have high hopes I broke his nose."

Paige stood expectantly as Cade drew closer. He touched the brim of his hat in greeting. "Morning, Captain."

"Jarvis." Parker cleared his throat. "Ms. Bryant tells me you have a theory about this break-in and an attack on her last night. Care to come to my office and discuss your conclusions?"

"Sure, if you want. All the details, except for what we found here this morning, have already been reported. The trouble started with the supposed accident that forced me off the road while I was on my way to Austin. State Troopers have all that info, plus there's a report to the local sheriff about what took place at Ms. Bryant's house. I was planning on stopping by to advise you about that in person. As you can see, we got a little sidetracked."

The older man leaned closer and began speaking far more quietly. "She says you agree there's a likely connection to several major crimes."

"Yes, sir, I do. I still can't prove anything but I expect to, eventually." He pointed toward her office. "The main thing is getting that skull ID and seeing if we can connect the victim to Captain Pike's murder."

"I sure hope you can. Keep me informed." Captain Parker looked to Paige. "And see that you keep a close eye on her, too. I don't like that bruise one bit."

As soon as Paige saw how apologetic the younger Ranger looked, she spoke up. "It wasn't Cade's fault. It happened before anybody knew I was being personally threatened." A smile began to lift the corners of her mouth. "I told you. I handled myself just fine."

"I'll say she did," Cade agreed. "I think I may have seriously underestimated the courage of our forensic artist."

To Paige's relief, that assessment of her character brought a smile back to the captain's leathery face. "I definitely agree with you there."

She was still basking in their mutual praise when Cade added, "However, I think her stubborn nature may be a problem in this case."

Paige's jaw dropped. "What?"

"She wouldn't let me sleep on her sofa last night so I had to camp in my truck to keep an eye on her." Cade kept smiling as if he and Parker were privy to some man-to-man secret that she'd never comprehend. "I figured it would be smart to put her up in a motel here in town, at least until she finishes the current job. That way, I'll be able to watch her better."

"I'll authorize whatever you need," the captain said. "Just do it. And see that there's a detailed report of all your suspicions, however far-fetched, on my desk ASAP. We can fill in the blanks later."

"Yes, sir." Cade touched a finger to the brim of his hat in an informal salute. "I suggest we include that dog of hers, too, since she won't be going home at night to take care of it."

Paige didn't realize she'd been holding her breath till the captain said, "Okay," and it all whooshed out at once. Max was going to be safe. Given the events of the past twenty-four hours, that was all she could hope for.

See? she thought, feeling for a fleeting moment like that confused, frightened ten-year-old who had failed her sister. *I can be trusted to care for something precious. I can. I really can.*

Max didn't care how inept she'd been in the past. He accepted her just as she was. Her only real wish was that others, such as her estranged parents, could one day be as forgiving, as tolerant.

And she needed God's forgiveness, too, Paige added. *He must be so disappointed in me. It's so sad for my family, never knowing what became of Amy.*

That solemn thought made Paige shiver. She knew the statistics. In the U.S. alone, 800,000 children a year were abducted or simply disappeared. Most were taken by relatives and eventually found alive but there were always a hundred or so who were held for ransom or killed, or both, usually within hours of their disappearance. Those remaining few who turned up years later, alive and well, were very rare.

Part of her wanted to continue to pray for answers

about her sister, while another part insisted that calling upon God was futile. After all, as she'd just concluded, He had to be as disappointed in her as she was in herself. Otherwise, why had He left her to grieve and wonder for so many years?

Something drew her attention back to Cade's face. To her astonishment, he was gazing at her as if he was not only reading her thoughts, but also sympathized. That was impossible, of course. Still, it was comforting to see so much tenderness in his eyes and to sense their almost spiritual connection.

That's because he doesn't know what I'm guilty of, she argued silently.

And, given their promised short time together, he never would. Not if she had any say in the matter.

SEVEN

Cade would have preferred to remain at headquarters and play a bigger part in the vandalism investigation. If he hadn't had Paige to worry about, he would never have insisted that they leave the premises and go to breakfast.

They were back in less than fifteen minutes. Since neither had wanted to leave the dog locked in the cab of her truck, they'd picked up their food at a drive-thru and then quickly returned to the lot behind her office.

Cade let down the tailgate to use as both a bench and dining table. Max stationed himself at their feet, panting and salivating copiously.

"I see now why you insisted we take your truck," he said wryly. "You were afraid all that dog drool in mine would freak me out. Right?"

"Well…"

He tossed the sheepdog a scrap of fried egg from his sandwich and heard its jaws snap shut. "Boy, I'm glad I didn't try to hand that to him. A guy could lose a finger."

Paige laughed. "Not really. He may be shy but he's

gentle." Her voice became a coo. "Aren't you, Max? Yes, you are. You're such a good boy."

"Do you think he understands a word you're saying?"

"I know he responds to kindness. He was afraid of his shadow when I first brought him home. All he wanted to do was slink around and try to hide. It was hilarious watching him trying to shimmy under the bed."

"Well, sure. He was shaved bare, right? I don't blame him for wanting to lay low till his fur grew back."

"Actually, he'd been terribly abused and neglected. The minute I laid eyes on him at the shelter I knew I couldn't go home without him."

"He seems to have pretty good manners. At least he's not jumping all over us to get at our food."

"I had to teach him everything from scratch, as if he were still a puppy. A *really* big one," Paige said with a grin. "He's basically civilized now, although he does forget his manners once in a while." She sobered. "That was why I went looking for him last night. I assumed he'd snuck out of the backyard and gotten into mischief."

"I really am sorry I wasn't able to come up with any concrete clues," Cade said. "Now that this has happened we shouldn't have any trouble getting authorization for a full team to go over your yard again."

"Speaking of that, look." Paige gestured with her plastic cup. "Some of the techs are pulling out of my studio. Maybe we'll be able to get to work on it soon."

"Don't hold your breath."

"Thanks heaps."

"Hey, I just call 'em the way I see 'em." He reached

into his jacket pocket in response to the ringing of a cell phone. "Excuse me for a sec?"

Flipping open the phone, Cade said, "Jarvis."

"Daniel here. Where are you?"

"Still in Austin. This may take a little longer than we'd planned. Everything okay?"

"Not exactly. I'm headed your way right now to speak with the governor. Hank Zarvy, the chairman of the Alamo Planning Committee, got a phone call warning him to call off the whole celebration for the 175th anniversary of the Battle of the Alamo or there'd be dire consequences. His words, not mine."

"Do you think this is connected to the threats we got before?"

"Probably. We're proceeding along those lines."

"Did anybody trace the call?"

"Couldn't. It came from a disposable phone."

Glancing at Paige, Cade noted that she was paying very close attention to his conversation. That was enough to keep him from actually mentioning the Lions of Texas again and giving her more cause for worry. At least for the present.

In his mind, however, he was certain the Lions had to be behind their recent troubles. All he and his fellow Rangers had to do was connect the dots, prove it and start making arrests. That couldn't happen soon enough to suit him.

"All right," Cade said. "When you get here, stop by headquarters and pick me up. I want to go with you to see Governor Kingston."

"Why?"

Paige was still watching him, clearly attempting to

read his thoughts. Rather than let her draw the conclusion that he intended to abandon her, he explained, "Because I want to include our forensic artist in the meeting."

As he bid his fellow ranger goodbye and ended the call, Cade's smile blossomed and rested on Paige. "You up for a field trip, lady?"

"You meant it? You're taking me with you to see the *governor?*"

"That was my intention." He noticed that she was trying to brush dog hair off her jeans.

"I can't go dressed like this. And what about Max? I already told you. I am *not* leaving him alone. Not after last night."

Chuckling, Cade couldn't help thinking how naive she seemed at times like these. "I'm sure he can stay with us, even when we go into the governor's office. After all, he'll have a Ranger escort."

Paige glanced down at her casual outfit once again. "I won't embarrass you?"

Although he could tell she was serious, he couldn't keep a straight face. "You might, if you jumped on the furniture or slid down the fancy banisters. Otherwise, I think you'll do fine, just as you are."

"Thank you," she said softly.

To Cade's surprise, it looked as if there was moisture glistening in her eyes, making them seem even greener than usual. He'd been to see the governor so often that doing so was commonplace to him. Apparently, being invited to officially visit a head of state was a big deal to the pretty artist.

All Cade could think to say was, "You're welcome."

* * *

Paige was glad she'd have the short trip to occupy her mind for the morning because just sitting there and waiting for a gang of strangers to finish dissecting her sanctuary, piece by piece, was extremely trying.

Although she'd been assured that the safe had not been breached, she'd still worn herself to a frazzle pacing up and down the sidewalks that crisscrossed the complex. A few times she'd even considered ducking out of the line of sight of the Ranger who was monitoring her every move as if she were a dangerous felon. Logic—and pain from the bruise on her arm—had kept her from being so foolish. After all, it wasn't Cade's fault that someone was posing threats and he was stuck with watching out for her.

That's exactly what's going on, Paige reminded herself. If she weren't in jeopardy he wouldn't be paying nearly this much attention to her. She knew that from experience. When they'd originally met in San Antonio, he'd barely bothered to offer more than a polite hello.

Truth to tell, when he'd arrived at her studio the evening before, she doubted he'd even recognized her. That conclusion made her smile. She'd recently had her long hair layered and had gotten contact lenses, so maybe he had been a bit surprised, assuming he'd noticed the changes at all.

A white pickup truck similar to Cade's pulled into the lot and stopped. As Paige watched, he jogged over to it and greeted the other Ranger who was driving. She was already on her way to join them when Cade motioned her over.

"This is Lieutenant Daniel Boone Riley," he said. "Daniel, meet Paige Bryant."

The darker-haired Ranger tipped his hat. "We've met. Nice to see you, ma'am."

"You, too, lieutenant. Your parents must have been avid history buffs to name you after Daniel Boone," Paige said, extending her hand and shaking his. "Good thing they didn't admire Socrates or Napoleon, huh?"

"You have no idea how thankful I am," Daniel replied.

Paige was pleased when everyone shared a laugh. She was as at ease with this Ranger as she was with Cade—maybe more so—because she was starting to really care what Ranger Jarvis thought of her. That was silly, of course, yet she couldn't seem to help herself. When he had insisted that she looked good enough to visit the governor, just as she was, he'd won her over in a big way. It had been a long, long time since she'd felt that totally accepted by anyone. It didn't matter that the hang-up was hers, it still existed.

"So, shall I hop in the back with Max?" she asked with a broad grin.

When both Rangers practically gasped, Paige giggled. "I know, I know. It's not chivalrous to put the woman in the back of the truck while the menfolk ride up front. I was just offering so I could keep Max out of trouble."

"I thought he was used to riding in a truck," Cade replied.

"He is. In the cab next to me like he did this morning." She was still laughing. "Sorry. I guess I'm more keyed-up than I thought. I giggle when I'm tense. Or tired. Or hungry. Or whatever."

Cade grinned at her as he opened and held the passenger door to Daniel's truck. "That's good to know. I'd hate to think you were about to lose it. Go ahead. Climb in."

As soon as Paige started to step up into the pickup, however, the shaggy dog pushed past and jumped in ahead of her. She glanced at Cade. "You might want to keep him on a shorter lead. He doesn't have his driver's license yet. I've been giving him lessons but he's a slow learner."

Cade reeled in the misbehaving dog, commenting aside to his fellow Ranger. "If she's teaching him, he'll never pass the test. I know. I followed her to work this morning so I know how crazy she drives."

Feigning disapproval, Paige took a playful swipe at Cade and landed a mock punch on his shoulder, immediately ruing her imprudence. His muscles were rock-solid. And he was starting to look at her as if she'd just hugged him instead of hitting him. At least that was the way she interpreted his expression.

"I think we should take two vehicles the way we did this morning," she said quickly. "That will give you guys a chance to talk business in private." Her eyebrows arched. "I don't want to accidentally overhear too much and get into more trouble than I'm already in."

When Cade rolled his eyes and said, "That'll be the day," she couldn't help laughing in spite of her ongoing uneasiness. Whatever results this case eventually brought, she knew she'd never regret getting to know Cade Jarvis.

As a matter of fact, she decided, turning and starting toward her own truck over the Rangers' objections, there was no way she'd be able to forget working with him. Not if she lived to be a hundred.

Daniel led the procession while Paige followed in her truck, giving Cade an opportunity to relax.

"You seem to be taking this whole situation with that woman a lot more seriously than I'd expected," Daniel said after Cade sighed audibly. "Why?"

"It's a long story."

"We've got fifteen minutes, at least. If you're going to talk, you'd better do it before your artist gets within earshot again."

"She's not my artist. She's *our* artist."

"Not judging by the way you two were carrying on. I'd heard tales that Paige Bryant was so serious she never cracked a smile, let alone laughed. And there you were, trading jokes and kidding around like old friends."

"I have no idea what you're talking about," Cade insisted, pausing to check the side mirror and make sure she was still in place behind them. "We hardly know each other."

"That doesn't change a thing. So, tell me what's been going on here? I saw the lab boys swarming all over. What I don't get is how this all ties in with Captain Pike." He frowned as he glanced at Cade. "Care to enlighten me?"

By the time Cade had related the details of his recent experiences, including those involving Paige, Daniel was scowling and glancing at her truck in his rearview mirror. "Does she have any idea how much trouble she may be in?"

"I doubt it. She tends to be so focused on her work she isn't really aware of much else."

"Okay," Daniel said, nodding. "What's plan A?"

"Long gone. I'm up to at least plan D, if not further. Every time I think I've got the situation under control, something else happens. So far, they've run me off the road, scared her half to death—twice—and trashed her studio. That doesn't leave much else."

"Except serious injury to her person. How badly was she hurt last night?"

"Bad enough to leave a bruise the size of some guy's meaty fist, and more. I can tell her shoulder hurts, too, judging by the way she favors it, but she's not about to admit it or see a doctor. That's why I've arranged to have her move into Austin, at least until this case is settled."

"Then what?" Daniel asked.

"Beats me. Once she models the face and we can put a name to the vic, she should be in the clear."

"Okay. If you say so. I sure don't like the idea of a connection to the Lions. They're too powerful for a regular citizen to mess with. Look what happened to the captain."

"Paige isn't just a citizen and neither was Greg," Cade argued. "They're a part of the Texas Rangers. We can't do anything for Greg except find his murderer, but I don't intend to let anything happen to Paige."

"I hope you can keep that promise."

"Yeah. Me, too." Cade nodded slowly, pensively, as he glanced in the side mirror of Daniel's truck to make sure she was still following.

For an instant, when he didn't see her because she'd

dropped behind another car, his heart nearly stopped. He swiveled to look directly. There she was. *Praise the Lord!*

"Calm down, man," the other Ranger said. "I've been keeping an eye on her. She's fine."

As Cade watched, her old, blue truck seemed to swerve slightly. It began to slow and drop back. "Hold it. Something's wrong."

"What?"

"I don't know," Cade shouted. "Pull over before we get too far ahead of her."

Due to heavy afternoon traffic, it was nearly impossible to find room to pass across all four lanes in a hurry. Cade continued to watch as they drew farther and farther away from Paige.

He could see that she'd made it safely to the shoulder. The question was, why had she stopped?

"Stupid tire," she grumbled, listening to the slapping of the rubber against the roadway. "What a time to pick to go flat."

The dog beside her started to pant and wiggle.

"No, Max. We're not going to get out and play." She held up her hand, flattened palm toward him, and said, "Sit. Stay."

Waiting for a clear space in the slowest lane, she quickly slid out of the truck and slammed the door behind her. One look told her the tire was flat all right. It looked as if part of the tread had come loose, the way the ones on big rigs sometimes did.

Paige frowned. Her father had been handy around cars but he'd had no time or inclination to pass his expertise on to his only remaining child.

She circled the rear of the truck and stood back, waiting for assistance. Texas was one of the friendliest places in the country. It wouldn't be long before she had the help she needed to change the flat.

"Providing the Rangers don't come back first," she muttered, hoping that would be the case. After all, this whole trip had been their idea. Therefore, she rationalized, it wasn't a big stretch of the imagination to blame her tire problem on them—even though it had been her decision to drive separately.

Despite the gathering gray cloud cover there was a bright glare. Shading her eyes, Paige peered at the traffic ahead. She could no longer see the white truck containing Cade and his buddy but she was certain they'd circle back as soon as they realized she'd had to stop.

Only then did it occur to her that the delay might make them late for their appointment with Governor Kingston. Terrific. Not only was she underdressed and with a dog, she was probably going to be the reason the Rangers didn't arrive promptly.

Looking in the opposite direction, Paige saw a black SUV stopped along the shoulder about fifty feet back. That vehicle may have also come into contact with whatever road hazard had flattened her tire, she reasoned. Just because she hadn't noticed anything lying on the highway didn't mean there hadn't been nails or glass or something like that. If so, it was probably amazing that there weren't more disabled cars pulling over to await repairs.

The SUV began to inch closer. Puzzled, Paige watched its approach. It didn't seem to be listing to one side the way her poor truck was. Maybe that driver had simply seen her tire blow and had had enough time to stop. That was okay, providing she got suitable help.

She made a cynical face. *The way my life has been going, the driver is probably a little old lady who can hardly pull herself into the driver's seat, let alone hop out and jack up my truck to change the tire.*

Enjoying the silly thought, she smiled and waved. The black vehicle stopped before it reached her. Should she walk back to explain? No. Surely her Rangers would return soon.

In the back of Paige's mind a suspicion began to grow. The roots of her hair tingled. There was something odd about the SUV, and its windows were tinted so dark she couldn't see in to allay any misgivings.

Her gaze darted to the lines of cars whizzing past. If a reckless driver came along and hit her parked truck, it could be shoved into the lanes of moving traffic and cause a terrible wreck. She'd watched enough TV news programs to know that getting passengers away from a disabled vehicle, if possible, was the smartest choice.

Turning, Paige jogged back to her pickup, approaching it on the passenger side. She was starting to open the door so she and her dog could wait farther up the landscaped, right-of-way incline when she heard the engine of the SUV rev. Its tires spun. Squealed.

Paige screamed, "Max! Come!" and leaped away with the end of his leash in her hand.

The dog reacted swiftly, not only running ahead but dragging her a few extra feet up the steep slope, as well.

She stumbled and landed on her hands and knees, crunching the dried stems and leaves of Texas bluebells and other wildflowers long past their prime. She rolled over. Her jaw dropped. Her eyes widened.

At the last second before a certain collision, the SUV had swerved into traffic instead of ramming her truck and slipped seamlessly into the flow of passing cars. Her heart was hammering so hard it almost drowned out the roar of the highway.

"Where's a cop when you need one?" she whispered, needing to hear the sound of her own voice to assure herself she was not merely stuck in another bad dream.

Should she try to get to her feet? Try to run farther away just to make sure they'd be safe? Maybe even go back to the truck to get her purse and cell phone?

No, she decided, doubting her legs would support her well if she tried. She and Max would sit right there and wait for those exasperating Rangers who had dragged her out here in the first place.

Her lower lip trembled. She bit it and fought down the urge to give in to panic. It had been many years since she'd felt this alone, this vulnerable.

Rangers like Cade tended to be so self-assured they were bossy, but she still couldn't think of a single other person she'd rather see approaching at that moment.

Where on earth was he?

EIGHT

Cade spotted the dusty blue truck in the distance long before he saw Paige. "There," he practically yelled, pointing out the window. "That has to be it."

"I know. Calm down. I'm sure she's fine."

"Well, *I'm* not sure. You wouldn't be so complacent if you'd been with her these past twenty-four hours." He set his jaw. "Where is she? I don't see anybody by the truck."

Daniel gestured. "Way up there on the bank. See? That's her." He started to slow and ease over onto the highway shoulder.

Cade hit the ground running before his companion had brought the truck to a full stop. He saw Paige try to stand, waver and plop back down.

Paige smiled as Cade approached, acting as though everything was fine. He wasn't fooled.

He held out his hand and she grasped it without a moment's hesitation. The instant he pulled her to her feet she was in his arms, clinging to him as if she were adrift in a storm at sea and he was her life preserver.

"We had to take the next off-ramp and circle back,"

he said, speaking with his cheek pressed against her hair. "What happened? Why did you stop?"

She eased away enough to look into his eyes and he saw fear in her gaze. "Didn't you see my truck? I had a blowout."

He'd been so focused on Paige that he hadn't bothered to take note of anything else. That was a clear indication that his priorities were becoming skewed and he didn't like admitting it, even to himself. Too bad it was so unmistakably true.

"If that's all that's wrong, then why are you shaking like a leaf? Are you cold?"

"No. There was another car. An SUV, I think. I thought the driver had stopped to help me but then he drove right at my truck, really fast, like he was going to *ram* it."

"Where were you when that happened?"

"Down there." She sniffled and pointed. "I'd gone back to get Max. We barely jumped clear in time. I was sure my truck was a goner. It's a good thing I wasn't still in it, even if they did miss."

Cade had an idea that her proximity to the truck had had little to do with the alleged attack—other than to thwart it. That conclusion chilled him to the bone. Chances were, if the driver of the SUV had been after Paige, as he assumed, it wouldn't have mattered where she was standing as long as she'd presented a clear target.

"Good thing you got out of the way," Cade said, pulling her against him for another brief hug before forcing himself to let go. "Otherwise, we might not be having this conversation. Come on. Let's go."

She'd swayed enough while he was speaking that Cade kept his hand on her arm as they started to descend the sloping right-of-way and return to join Daniel. He didn't intend to pause at her truck as they passed but she insisted.

"Wait. I need my purse. And I threw my overnight bag back in here, too. It'll only take a second."

"Okay. Hurry it up." Keeping one wary eye on the traffic, Cade stepped just far enough away from her to check her wheels. What he saw gave him chills. The left rear tire was flat, all right. And there was a crease in the metal rim that looked a lot like the damage a glancing bullet might cause.

He was hunkered down, using his pocket knife to probe for the projectile, when Paige peeked around the rear bumper at him. "What are you doing?"

"Nothing." Cade straightened, folded the knife and slipped it back into his pocket. "I'd hoped there'd be a clue in there but I didn't find anything."

"A clue? What kind of a clue?"

Instead of answering, he countered with another question. "Did you see or hear anything unusual just before you felt the flat?"

"Like what?"

"Like a loud bang or whistle. Anything that might explain why it looks like that wheel was shot."

"Shot? Are you *serious?*"

Cade nodded soberly. "Very. There's been another attack on you."

"That's ridiculous. How would anyone know I'm not at work? That's where I always am at this time of day."

"How? The same way they seem to have known

everything else," Cade said, reaching for her suitcase to relieve her of that burden. "Can you describe the car you say almost hit you?"

As they started to walk toward Daniel's idling truck, he put the suitcase in his outside hand and slipped an arm around her shoulders, staying on the traffic side for her defense.

"I don't know. It all happened so fast. It was an SUV. It was big. And black, and…"

Cade tightened his grip and stopped in his tracks. "What did you say?"

"It was a black SUV. I'd already told you that."

"No, you didn't. You never mentioned a color." He stared at her. "Think. Did you see any scrapes on the side of it when it went by?"

"I don't know."

Gazing into her wide-eyed expression he recognized the moment when she put two and two together. Her jaw gaped. "What…? What was the color of the one that forced you off the road?"

"Black," Cade said, "and judging by the damage to my truck, there has to be plenty showing on that other vehicle, too."

Paige closed her eyes for a few seconds, then opened them. "I was running away at the time so I didn't see it clearly when it passed by. I do think it had a bent frame around one headlight, though. The one closest to the shoulder of the highway."

Picking up the pace again he hustled her toward Daniel's waiting truck. "I never should have let you drive alone, no matter how much you insisted. Believe me, it won't happen again."

"Hey, don't go overboard. There's no real proof that this flat wasn't an accident. At least not yet."

"I don't have to see proof of an attack to recognize one. We'll call the State Troopers and have them impound your vehicle so it can be checked."

"Okay, but…"

"No buts. If you won't think of yourself, consider your value to the Rangers. We need your expertise."

"I'm not the only forensic artist in Texas."

"True. But you're very skilled and you also have the latest equipment at your fingertips. Or you did, until this morning. Besides, if we had to farm out this job it might take a lot longer."

"Then maybe it's not all about me. Maybe it's more *time* they're really after."

The logic behind her conclusion struck him as absolutely brilliant. "It may be! You're a genius. We need to look for some kind of time constraint."

"Such as?"

"I don't know. Maybe a big drug shipment or something like that." Cade shrugged. He wasn't certain of anything, but when Paige had mentioned timing, it had also occurred to him that there was one truly important event pending. The 175th anniversary celebration at the Alamo was coming in March.

Which conveniently happened to tie into Daniel's current reason for visiting the governor. The planning board had already been warned repeatedly that someone was going to interrupt those festivities, probably with violence, and now there had been another threat. The question was, how serious were they?

His jaw clenched. It was beginning to look as if the

skull was crucial to multiple investigations, but how? They already knew that the land on which the remains had been found was connected to the Lions of Texas. Captain Pike's murder was also tied to that gang, so it was highly possible that this victim's identity would lead to more evidence against the Lions. Other than stealing the skull outright, stopping or delaying Paige's work was the gang's only real option.

Which left the threats regarding the Alamo. As far as Cade was concerned, there was a good chance the Lions were behind those, too. Otherwise, why stall for time? What did they think Paige was going to discover? Or rather, *who?*

Paige gladly agreed to ride with the Rangers after they'd arranged for a tow truck to haul her pickup off the highway and deliver it to the Department of Transportation garage. By the time all that was accomplished, she was feeling a lot more like her old self.

To her delight, Cade had suggested that they could squeeze Max into the cab with them if he allowed the dog to sit at his feet. Paige occupied the middle of the seat, between the Rangers.

The sight of Max and Cade squashed into so small an area together was truly comical. "You sure you don't want to trade places with me?" she asked him.

"No. You're safer right where you are."

She giggled. "Okay. If you change your mind, let me know."

Max continued to wiggle happily until Cade was wearing more dog hair than Paige was, not to mention a little happy-dog drool on one knee.

"Thanks for the lift, guys," she said with a grin. "Guess I should have agreed to ride with you in the first place, huh?"

The expression on Cade's face was a cross between disgust and suppressed humor. "And I should have traded places with this mutt and climbed into the back where I'd be out of his reach. I'm going to have to borrow Daniel's currycomb to clean myself up before I dare let the governor see me."

His companion chuckled. "Yeah. And if I'd known I'd have so many passengers I might have parked this new truck and driven my old SUV. Good thing Rangers carry horse equipment as well as other gear." He glanced at Cade's clothing. "I've seen less hair on Captain Parker's head."

When Cade ordered "Hush," Paige giggled.

"It's okay," she said. "I'll never tell. We all know there isn't much left under his cattleman's hat. He makes up for it with that magnificent mustache, though."

"It's not as good as Max's," Cade countered. "Don't you ever comb this dog?"

"Of course I do. I could knit a sweater out of what I brush out."

"I think you missed a bunch. So nice of him to share it with me."

"Hey, you were the one who insisted we all had to stay together from now on. And that I couldn't sit by the door. Not that I mind, considering." She looked from one man to the other. "Where did you put my suitcase?"

"It's in the back," Daniel answered. "I figured it would be safer there than up here on the floor."

"You're probably right."

In the distance, she caught sight of the capitol building with its decorative marble columns and copper-clad dome. That was where she was going. Her. Paige Bryant. The person who preferred solitude and anonymity above all else was about to enter the seat of Texas government and meet the man who ran the state. That concept boggled her mind.

Given a choice, she'd almost rather have been back among the faded bluebells—if she hadn't also been in probable danger then, shivering when she remembered what Cade had said about his own accident and recalled the way the SUV had been pointed right at her.

Paige noted that Cade immediately cast her a quick glance so she made a point of smiling at him.

"Are you chilly?" he asked.

"No. I'm fine."

"You sure?"

"Positive," Paige replied. "Nobody has doused any lights, grabbed me from the bushes, trashed my possessions or tried to make roadkill out of me and Max for at least ten minutes. I'm just peachy."

The Rangers had little trouble gaining admittance at the capitol for their entire party, much to Paige's amazement. Because the dog had balked at entering a private elevator, she and Cade were climbing the sweeping, marble staircase with him, the way most tourists did, while Lieutenant Riley went on ahead to brief the governor.

"This place is beautiful," Paige whispered, awed. "So ornate and elegant."

"The building was originally finished in 1888, after

the first capitol burned to the ground. I remember not being very impressed when my father brought me here before the restoration in the 1990s. I think the preservation people did a great job, especially since they had to incorporate modern systems without changing the overall appearance of the place."

"Wow. No kidding." She craned her neck to gaze up at the red, Texas lone star inlaid inside the dome that topped the rotunda. "It's so beautiful."

"You live in Austin. Are you telling me you've never taken the tour of our own capital?"

"Nope. Never have. I kept meaning to but with work and all, I never seemed to get around to it."

"Well, when this case is closed, maybe you and I should come back and make like tourists. How about it?"

"Maybe." In the back of her mind she kept telling herself that the Ranger was just being polite, yet part of her couldn't help wishing he'd actually meant the offer.

Once they were done with the current case, everything would change. She knew that. It always did. The last thing she wanted to do was see any investigation drag out longer than absolutely necessary. However, there was still a tiny voice in her mind urging her to make the most of this special time with Cade Jarvis and promising that there was nothing wrong with enjoying herself once in a while.

Paige smiled, turning away so he couldn't see how pleased she was to be in his company. The entire scenario was unbelievable. Here she was, walking up a marble staircase practically arm-in-arm with the most handsome Ranger in Texas, on her way to see Governor Kingston, and she'd even been allowed to bring her best four-legged friend along.

Life did not get much better—or stranger—than that.

NINE

Daniel was already deep in conversation with the stately, gray-haired Governor Kingston when Cade and Paige joined them and were quickly introduced.

Tall and well-dressed, as befitted his position, Kingston grinned at Paige. "My pleasure, ma'am. I don't often have such unique visitors." He shook hands with her and gestured toward one of the burgundy leather chairs. "Please, make yourself at home."

"Thank you."

"Ms. Bryant is directly involved in a case I'm pursuing," Cade explained when he noticed the governor's eyebrows arch questioningly in his direction. "She's our forensic artist. I've been assigned to keep her under close guard until her work is completed, so I brought her along."

"I see." Kingston smiled wryly. "Are there no other Rangers or Troopers available to look after her in your absence? If they're all that busy, maybe I need to see about funding the hiring of more."

Nobody had to tell Cade that his face was red. Not only could he feel the added warmth creeping up from his collar, his telling reaction was reaffirmed by the smug expressions on the other men.

"It's complicated," Cade said. "I—we—felt that it was best to keep this situation under wraps until we know more about who our adversaries are."

Kingston eyed him. "I thought that was clear?"

"We have no direct proof of a connection, as yet. It's just a theory."

"A good one, I trust."

"Yes, sir. If you want to discuss it in more depth, in private, I can take Ms. Bryant outside."

Daniel rescued him. "I don't believe there's anything more to add, Governor. I've given you the details of the threat, as Mr. Zarvy recalled them. The Rangers will do our best to protect you if you insist on going through with your plans to speak at the Alamo anniversary celebration, but it might be best if you thought about withdrawing."

"Nonsense. The lieutenant governor and I will both be there." He displayed a satisfied smile. "And, I'm pleased to tell you that we've recently gotten confirmation that the vice president will also attend."

Cade's eyes popped. "*The* vice president? Of the United States?"

"Yes," Kingston replied, grinning wider. "I consider it a great honor to have him with us on the podium. After all, the 175th anniversary of the Battle of the Alamo is a milestone. It's a fundamental part of Texas history."

Although Cade felt like cringing he kept his shoulders square, his jaw clenched. As if they didn't already have enough trouble, now they were going to have one more dignitary's welfare to worry about. Terrific.

Well, there was nothing he could do about it except execute his duties to the best of his ability. The rest was up to God. *And the U.S. Secret Service,* he added, stifling a grin. With all those branches of law enforcement involved, they'd probably end up tripping over each other by the time the celebration concluded.

Ideally, Cade thought, Paige would finish her reconstruction before then, the victim would be identified and that ID would lead them to making enough arrests that everyone in Texas would be considerably safer.

He huffed cynically at the turn of his imagination. When the Lions of Texas were involved, nothing was ever that simple. It seemed their favorite method of dealing with people who caused them trouble was to swat them like pesky mosquitoes.

Nothing like that was going to happen to Paige Bryant, he vowed. Especially not while he was on duty.

By the time Paige and the others got back to headquarters and they parted company with Lieutenant Riley, her office was no longer an active crime scene.

That was somewhat comforting until she set foot in what had once been her sanctuary. Now, not only could she see obvious damage to her computers and files, there was black fingerprint powder dusted over every usable surface. Her heart sank.

"I hardly know where to begin," she said.

"With the easy stuff. Come on. I'll help. You stand by the filing cabinets and I'll pass the folders to you. Then you'll be able to get to your computers and the safe without stepping on everything else."

Paige blew a noisy sigh. "Okay. I guess that's as good a plan as any."

"You're supposed to say, 'Thank you, Cade. You're the smartest guy in Texas.'"

"Oh?" She couldn't help but smile when she saw his droll expression. The man could go from looking as if he could single-handedly whip a closet full of wildcats to being such a marshmallow that he'd be a pushover for anybody, even her.

"Okay, Ranger Jarvis. You are obviously the most brilliant Ranger there ever was and you should definitely be promoted to chief as soon as possible."

"You mean senior captain. But I get the gist." Chuckling, he hung his jacket over the back of a chair, then carefully crossed the room to the filing cabinets. "You don't need to go that far. Let's just say I plan to continue working my way up and maybe someday be worthy of leading the Rangers as ably as Captain Parker. I'd like to be half the man Gregory Pike was. He'd have made a great senior captain."

"Losing him was a terrible shock to all of us." Paige approached and briefly laid her hand on Cade's forearm to offer moral support. "Poor Corinna told me her father was all the family she had."

"The captain's replacement, Ben Fritz, has been a lot of comfort to her since then."

"Good. I didn't have a chance to really get to know her well," Paige said. "I wish I could have helped more."

"Drawing that sketch of her stalker was plenty. All any of us can do is keep putting clues together till we have answers." Cade stooped and began to pick up scattered folders, righting them to help her read the tabs as he handed them over.

Paige began to automatically restore her records while her mind darted in a dozen different directions. "Nothing like this has ever happened to me before. That's why I think there must be a solid connection between all these attacks and the skull I'm going to be working on."

"Obviously," Cade said. "Trouble is, it's like looking at this jumble on the floor. The answers may be there, but right now they're so mixed up it's impossible to sort them out. If I can't make sense of it, nobody can."

"Oh, really?" Paige's eyebrows arched.

In response, his brown eyes sparkled and Paige was nearly lost in their appealing depths. "Never mind," she said, hoping she wasn't looking at him like a teenaged movie fan with a crush on a handsome star. "All I ask is that you keep me informed of anything new that might put me or Max in more jeopardy. Will you do that?"

When he nodded in affirmation, Paige thought she glimpsed a flash of emotion. It was so fleeting, so tenuous, she immediately doubted her conclusion. Cade was a rough, tough Texas Ranger, not some desk jockey whose biggest challenge was mowing his lawn on Saturdays. Rangers were men who faced death and danger all the time. They had a reputation for being able to wade into a perilous situation and defuse it with their mere presence. She'd heard so many stories to that effect that she didn't doubt most were true.

Without another word, Cade began to gather stacks of files into his arms and pile them on a table.

"*Now* what are you doing?"

"Making room for you," he said flatly. "Doing it the

other way is going to take too long. Sit down at your desk and see if your main computer needs repair while I pick up the rest of this stuff. That way, once we get the room straightened up, you'll be able to dive right back into your work."

"Very sensible," Paige said, realizing with chagrin that she may have bruised his ego when she'd teased about his crime-solving ability. "Look. I'm sorry if I sounded as though I was doubting you. I really am thankful you're here—for work reasons, of course."

"Of course." He began lounging with a hip against the edge of the table, arms crossed and peering at her as if she were a rare insect being examined under a microscope.

Paige folded her own arms and faced him. This was a standoff. He wanted her to admit that she liked having him around and she was loathe to do so. Nevertheless, she did feel she owed him honesty. "I was—I am—glad you're taking time from your busy schedule to assist me," she said, making a face when he started to give her that lazy, Texas grin of his.

He touched the brim of his hat. "Yes, ma'am. My pleasure, Miss Paige."

"I told you…"

Before she could finish complaining he shook with subdued chuckles and relaxed his stance. "I know, I know. Sounds too much like I'm talkin' to your granny." He bent to gather more files. "So, tell me a little about your family. Do you have a granny?"

"Everybody has grandmothers," Paige informed him. "Mine don't happen to be living but I remember a little about one of them. She was a dear. A tiny thing with a temper that made my grandpa cringe."

"Ah, you must take after her."

"I beg your pardon?" Ready to take offense, she was surprised to see the twinkle in Cade's eyes. He'd been teasing and she'd almost missed it because she'd been taking him too seriously.

"Maybe you're right. Maybe I can be a little prickly at times," she said. "I spend so much time working alone it's apparently hard for me to accept the fact that I might need anyone's help."

"I don't care if you have as many thorns as a giant saguaro," Cade said, maintaining his grin. "You're not going to get rid of me. Not as long as I think you need me around."

"Is that a threat or a promise?" Paige asked.

She had to smile when he replied, "Both."

Cade would gladly have driven anywhere to pick up whatever Paige needed to continue her work. Regrettably, although she had the facial recognition and reconstruction programs on disc, she couldn't reload them until her damaged desktop computer was repaired or replaced. She also informed him the 3-D laser scanner was broken and she needed it to fabricate a composite reconstruction of the skull on which to build the clay face. With her laser workstation down and obtaining a replacement at least a week away or more, they were totally stymied.

"How about having some of that work done in San Antonio?" Cade asked. "Can't they make the same kind of scan?"

"Maybe, if they have a scanner that's compatible with

my systems or if somebody ran a complete MRI before you brought me the skull. I'd still want to double-check a mockup before I trusted its accuracy. My job may look artistic but it's also hard science."

He arched a brow and glanced at her studio. "You can't even start when everything's such a mess. If another lab can eliminate one or two steps for you, you should be glad."

"I know. I'm just used to doing things my way."

Amused, Cade grinned at her. "Yeah. I got that impression."

His mood improved even more when she sighed in resignation and smiled back at him. "So, since I'm currently computerless, what do we do next?"

"First, we get you settled at the motel. I've arranged for a suite with connecting doors and locks on both sides, in case you don't trust me."

"I've already trusted you with my life," Paige said. "Besides, I'll have Max to guard me. You did get permission for him to be in my room, didn't you?"

"Of course. Max is just as important as you are." To Cade's delight, that comment obviously pleased her.

"I can't argue since I feel the same." Paige wiggled her fingers in the sheepdog's thick fur. "If that crazy driver had hit my truck when I stopped, and Max had still been inside…"

"Don't dwell on it," Cade advised. "You need to concentrate on the future, not the past. Getting your job done without making any more mistakes is the most important thing right now."

"I never make mistakes. Ask Captain Parker."

Cade quickly shook his head and explained, "I didn't

mean in regard to your work. I meant in your private life. You're not to go anywhere alone. Don't even leave your motel room without me. Promise." It wasn't a question. He also didn't receive an answer. "Paige? Did you hear me?"

"Yes. And I can't say I like the idea. I appreciate your concern but I'm used to doing things for myself—by myself."

"And you will again, once your life gets back to normal. Right now, I need you to give your word you'll listen to my advice."

"I'm listening."

Cade had a niggling feeling that she was choosing her words carefully to give an acceptable impression rather than make a promise she might later want to break.

He stepped in front of her and gently gripped her shoulders for emphasis as he spoke. "It's this way, Ms. Bryant. You will either promise to follow my orders or I'll be forced to barricade your door and windows at night to keep you in your room. Is that clear?"

Her eyes sparked with emerald fire. Her lips were pressed into a thin line. She glared at him. "You wouldn't dare."

"Try me." As far as Cade was concerned it was more important to guarantee her safety than to curry her favor. If she got mad at him, so be it. His duty was to protect her—even from herself. "And if I were you, I'd make this decision very carefully."

Paige gaped. "I think you're serious."

"Deadly serious."

"What happened to those famous Texas Ranger powers of persuasion?"

Cade chanced a smile in the hopes it would help temper her indignant attitude. "I'm using them right now. How am I doing?"

"Lousy," she said, although the corners of her mouth twitched as if she were trying to suppress a grin.

"Then I guess I'll have to try harder," Cade told her. "In the meantime, grab your overnight stuff and your purse and let's go. There's nothing more you can do here and you must be exhausted." He stifled a yawn. "I know I am."

"In a way that's my fault because I kept you up half the night," Paige said, looking chagrined. "Okay. You win. This time. Just remember, I do not take orders well."

"Then let me put it this way. Shall we go, ma'am?"

"Delighted," she said, picking up her light burdens and snapping Max's leash to the ring on his collar.

Cade double-checked to make sure the studio door was closed and locked, then followed Paige down the hallway to the rear exit. Everything in and around the administrative complex was well lit and the locks on the outer doors had been reprogrammed, as had Paige's. Plus, there were Rangers and Troopers practically everywhere during daylight hours, so he wasn't too worried. Yet.

Deep in thought, he was pondering how best to arrange their nightly accommodations to provide the most protection for Paige as he followed her outside.

"Do you have your new key card?" he asked.

"Yes. I wish I knew what's become of my old keys. I never did find them. They probably fell out of my purse at home."

"Well, we're not going there to look for them," Cade said, assuming they'd been stolen but deciding to keep that conclusion to himself. The arch of her eyebrows told him he'd better learn to phrase his orders with a bit more finesse where Paige was concerned. "I mean, surely you won't need them with the new lock."

"I suppose you're right."

What he wanted to say in addition would not have helped the situation so he kept his mouth shut. Since her truck had not been returned, he pointed to the spot where his was parked beneath a clump of cottonwoods. "You can put Max in the front seat as long as he sits by the door."

"That means I'd be stuck in the middle again?" She made a face.

"If you don't like that idea, then make him stay on the floor the way I did when we rode with Daniel," Cade said, a little put out by the clear implication that she didn't want to sit in the middle, close to him, when it hadn't seemed to bother her to do so before.

Watching her flounce around to the passenger side of the pickup and reach for the door handle, he hesitated. Normally, he'd have circled the truck and politely held the door for her. Considering the prickly mood she was in, however, he decided it was wiser to stay where he was.

Standing next to the cottonwoods, Paige began to jerk on the door handle. "It won't open. I told you it was too damaged."

"Then come back around and get in on this side. There's nothing wrong with this door," Cade said.

He saw her pause. Look down. Apparently tug on the

leash as she urged, "Come on, Max. What's the matter with you?"

That was enough to set off Cade's internal warning system. He peered at her over the hood of the truck. "What's wrong?"

"I don't know. He's…"

Suddenly, Paige tilted as if she were off-balance. She gasped and leaned to one side, screeching, "No! Let go!"

Cade's heart leaped. Though he didn't see any antagonist, he was nevertheless racing to her rescue in a split second. One boot sole slipped on the pavement. He had his gun drawn by the time he rounded the front bumper and saw Paige clearly. She was seated on the ground. The leash was wrapped around her ankles.

"The *dog* tripped you?"

"No!" Shouting, she pointed. "Look! That guy just stole my bag."

Cade saw two problems. One, there was no way he dared shoot within the confines of the state complex. And two, the culprit was already clear across the parking lot and still running.

He reluctantly holstered his sidearm and reached for Paige. "Are you all right? Did he hurt you?"

She arose without help and dusted dry leaf litter off her jeans. "No. I'm fine." She scowled at Cade. "Why would anybody want to steal my clothes?"

"I don't think it was your clothes they were after. I think they may have thought you were taking work home with you."

"Like the skull? Well, they're going to be really disappointed," she replied with a grimace. "All they got were a few T-shirts and my jammies. I didn't even remember to pack the sketch I made of my prowler. It's still sitting at home on my kitchen table."

"Don't worry. You can always draw another picture. We'll go shopping and buy you some new clothes after you're settled at the motel, too." He ushered her around to the driver's side and opened the door. "Get in and let's roll."

"What's your hurry?"

Although he could tell she was far more concerned than she appeared, he chose to speak plainly. "Because that guy may not be working alone. The less time you spend out in the open, the harder it will be for anyone else to get at you."

"I thought you were going to protect me."

"Yeah." Cade would have gladly kicked himself if he'd been double-jointed enough to do it. "And if this is the best I can do, it looks like you'd be better off with somebody else."

To his surprise and chagrin she stuck up for him. "Don't be silly. I don't want anyone else. I want you."

He was just about to figuratively pat himself on the back when Paige added, "Besides, one Texas Ranger underfoot every second of every day is about all I can stand."

TEN

Cade had officially reported the theft of Paige's overnight bag, then kept in touch by phone and radio to follow the investigation on their way to the motel. Since the thief had left behind no clues other than a vague description, there was nothing anyone could do except check the surveillance cameras around the complex and see if the techs could come up with a plate number for his getaway vehicle. If they could, it might prove to be important—especially if it happened to be attached to a black, dented SUV.

"What now?" Paige was standing in the middle of her modest motel room and eyeing the open door.

"Dinner and shopping. You need clothes, remember?"

To his chagrin she stood firm, shook her head and crossed her arms. "I hate to shop."

Eyeing her from head to toe, Cade smiled. "Then how are you going to replace your stolen stuff?"

The teasing, amused expression she displayed in reply was telling. His eyes narrowed. "Oh, no, you don't. I am not going into a store and buying women's clothes for you."

"Why not? I thought Rangers were fearless."

Cade could tell she was enjoying his discomfiture far too much. "I'd rather face a gang of armed cattle rustlers than be seen shopping for a woman."

"Chicken."

He thought seriously of teasing her back by making a clucking noise, then decided it would be best not to encourage her. She seemed able to come up with plenty of quips without his help and the more seriously she took their situation, the better.

"I don't see any feathers on me," Cade replied, still so concerned for her that it tied his gut in a knot. He reached for her hand and clasped it gently. "Look. I know this whole business is tough on you. I wish it weren't. But there's nothing I can do to change what's happening except keep a close eye on you and trust God to take care of the rest."

Paige rolled her eyes and made a silly face. "Don't mind me. I tend to find humor in even the most dire situations. That helps me cope with the difficulties I meet every day in my job. I really am taking your warnings to heart."

"You must have been the biggest joker in class when you were a kid."

As he watched, her gaze darkened and a somberness flowed over her that was unlike anything he'd ever seen her display. Gone was any trace of a smile. The depth of her emotion was unfathomable. Instead of speaking, she merely shook her head and pulled her hand from his grasp, then picked up Max's leash and headed for the door.

"Paige? What is it? What did I say wrong?"

GET 2 BOOKS

IF YOU ENJOY A ROMANTIC SUSPENSE STO
that reflects solid, traditional values, then you'll like *Love Inspired® Suspense* novels. These are contemporary tales of intrigue and romance featuring Christian characters facing challenges to their faith…and their lives!

We'd like to send you two *Love Inspired Suspense* novels absolutely free. Accepting them puts you under no obligation to purchase any more books.

HOW TO GET YOUR
2 FREE BOOKS AND 2 FREE GIFTS

1. Return the reply card today, and we'll send you two *Love Inspired Suspense* novels, absolutely free! We'll even pay the postage!

2. Accepting free books places you under no obligation to buy anything, ever. The two books have combined cover prices of at least $11.00 in the U.S. and at least $13.00 in Canada, but they're yours to keep, free!

3. We hope that after receiving your free books you'll want to remain a subscriber, but the choice is yours—to continue or cancel, any time at all!

EXTRA BONUS

You'll also get two free mystery gifts! (worth about $10)

FREE!

Return this card today to get
2 FREE BOOKS and 2 FREE GIFTS!

Love Inspired®
SUSPENSE
RIVETING INSPIRATIONAL ROMANCE

YES! Please send me 2 FREE *Love Inspired® Suspense* novels, and 2 free mystery gifts as well. I understand I am under no obligation to purchase anything, as explained on the back of this insert.

About how many NEW paperback fiction books have you purchased in the past 3 months?

❏ 0-2
FC5D

❏ 3-6
FC5P

❏ 7 or more
FC5Z

❏ I prefer the regular-print edition
123/323 IDL

❏ I prefer the larger-print edition
110/310 IDL

FIRST NAME	LAST NAME

ADDRESS

APT.#

CITY

STATE/PROV.

ZIP/POSTAL CODE

(LISUS-2F-11)

BUSINESS REPLY MAIL
FIRST-CLASS MAIL   PERMIT NO. 717   BUFFALO, NY

POSTAGE WILL BE PAID BY ADDRESSEE

THE READER SERVICE
PO BOX 1867
BUFFALO NY 14240-9952

NO POSTAGE
NECESSARY
IF MAILED
IN THE
UNITED STATES

"Nothing," she replied flatly. "Let's go get this over with."

As Cade followed her to his truck, he stayed on full alert while also mulling over her reaction to his innocent mention of her childhood. That had to be the key to her personality quirks, he reasoned. Once he learned what she'd gone through in her youth he should be able to understand what made her tick. And then he'd be able to anticipate what she might or might not do in a difficult situation.

Tonight, after he got her settled and locked safely away in her room, he'd research her past as he'd intended in the first place. Anything he found out would be of less importance than the effect it was having on her as an adult. Whatever the problem had been, at least he'd have an idea how to keep from putting his boot in his mouth again.

And maybe, just maybe, he'd also be able to help her overcome the immense sadness he'd just witnessed. Above all, Cade wanted to lift that unspoken burden.

Why do you care so much? he asked himself. There was no satisfactory answer. At least not one he was willing to accept. The fact that Paige Bryant's well-being had become so important to him in such a short time was disquieting enough.

Time dragged by for Paige. She'd never much cared for shopping, and being forced to replace her clothing on the spur of the moment was anything but pleasant. Nevertheless, she picked out a few basics and hurried outside, finding Cade and Max stationed beside the door to the small dress shop in the strip mall, waiting like two oddly matched sentries.

He squared his broad shoulders the moment he spied her. "Did you get everything?"

"Enough to make do," she replied. "I keep a hairbrush and lipstick in my purse so all I'll need is a toothbrush and I'll be fine."

"We can get one of those from the motel office," he said, taking her arm and starting to hustle her back to his truck. "Come on."

She twisted free. "Slow down, cowboy. What's the rush? Did you see someone else who looked suspicious or are you always this pushy?"

"Both," Cade answered. "It's getting so I imagine villains in every shadow."

Falling into step beside him, Paige added, "Or behind every tree?" She was instantly sorry she'd chided him because the look on his face became so poignant it was almost heartrending. He really did care. And she shouldn't have made a joke about his efforts.

"Sorry," she said with a lopsided grin. "I didn't mean to hurt your feelings. I was just kidding around. Remember? I'm a real funny lady."

"Yeah, I know." As they approached the truck he hit a remote button that unlocked the doors, then helped her into the truck with her packages.

Paige did her best to scoot across the seat and get Max out of his way as Cade slid behind the wheel. As soon as he started the engine she asked, "Could we pick up a pizza to eat back at the motel?"

"Sounds fine to me," Cade said. "You're right about keeping a low profile. The less you're out in public, the better. It might even be a good idea to skip church on Sunday."

"No problem. I seldom go to church, even when nobody's trying to scare me to death."

"Really? Why?"

"It's a long story," she said with a sigh.

"I've got all evening."

She could tell by his quizzical expression that he was expecting her to explain. No way was that going to happen. Not now. Not ever.

Forcing herself to smile she looked over at him and said sweetly, "Nobody has enough time or patience to listen to my long, boring life story. Believe me, you don't want to get me started."

"Okay. Have it your way."

If I could have it my way, Paige thought, *I'd know what had happened to my sister all those years ago.*

She simply said, "Thanks," instead of what was really on her mind. She sighed and closed her eyes for the space of a few heartbeats, picturing her long-lost sister and feeling the weight of that one, terrible mistake bearing down upon her.

A solitary tear spilled out and slid down her cheek. Paige averted her face and swiped away the telltale drop. What was wrong with her? Why were her emotions so close to the surface of late? Was it the fear? The tension?

No, she decided. She might be overtired but she'd been that way before and it hadn't made her weep, nor had it caused her to keep recalling Amy.

A flash of insight nearly took Paige's breath away. She stared at Cade. *He* made the difference. For the first time in many years she was with someone in whom she yearned to confide. What a shock. And what a surprise, although certainly not a welcome one.

She'd been doing just fine without opening up to anybody—except Max—and he was a safe confidant only because he couldn't talk, couldn't offer the sympathy she knew she didn't deserve.

That was her basic problem, Paige realized. Cade was not only a Ranger, he was a member of their unsolved crimes unit. If he ever learned about her sister's case he would be highly likely to want to look into the kidnapping, and there were others who were far more deserving than she was.

I must be crazy, Paige told herself. All this time, she'd believed she was hoping for a breakthrough, yet now that she was facing that possibility, she was terrified. Why?

Because I know Amy must be dead, she answered truthfully for the first time since childhood. That realization tore at her heart as if someone had actually stabbed her. She crossed her arms and hugged herself tightly, hoping she could maintain the stolid self-control that had gotten her through in the past.

What she wanted to do was fall into Cade's arms again, the way she had when he'd rescued her from the side of the highway. Instead, she averted her face so the Ranger wouldn't suspect she was silently weeping.

It didn't take Cade long to access the UCIT cold-case files once he was alone in his room with his laptop. To his chagrin, he didn't find anything listed that mentioned a Paige Bryant. That meant he'd have to dig deeper, perhaps beyond the most recent years. His instincts told him she was hiding something. All he had to do was figure out what.

If the event—or events—concerning Paige had been newsworthy and had occurred in this part of Texas, there was one man who might remember. His father, Jacob. And once he had a lead, it would be easier for Cade to track down pertinent details.

Taking a chance, he phoned the former Trooper. "Hi, Dad. I didn't wake you, did I?"

"Naw. I was just watchin' one of those cop shows that always make me mad 'cause they get the procedures all wrong. How are you?"

"Fine. I'm still on that case in Austin I told you about. Everything okay at the ranch?"

"Fine. What's goin' on, son?"

"I'll fill you in when we get together for Thanksgiving, if not before. In the meantime, I was wondering if you could give me a little help? Does the name Paige Bryant ring a bell?"

"Isn't she that artist that reconstructs faces?"

"Yes. I don't mean what she does now, I mean in the past. I thought maybe…"

"Bryant, Bryant. Hmm. I do seem to recall a couple of little girls by that name. One of 'em went missing back when I was still a green Trooper. Sad case. We never did find a single lead to the whereabouts of that child."

"About how long ago was that?"

"You were in junior high or high school, I think."

Cade's brow furrowed. "I think I do remember something about that case. You were pretty upset at the time."

"Yeah. Cute little thing she was. Only I don't think her sister was named Paige. Could be wrong about that. It's been a long time."

"Okay. Thanks. If you remember anything else, give me a call, okay?"

"Sure, son. Take care of yourself, now."

"I will."

Bidding his father goodbye, Cade began typing on his laptop. Not all the files from past cases had been entered into the active database so it was possible he'd have to find original paperwork if he hoped to learn more than whatever turned up in an internet search.

There was one other thing he could do first, he decided, entering his name and password to try to gain access to basic Ranger personnel files. Although unable to see every detail, in a few minutes he'd found what he was looking for. *Paige* was her middle name rather than her first. Dropping a name wasn't that unusual, yet it did tend to indicate that she didn't want to be readily identified by the casual observer.

He was far from that, Cade told himself. Although there was little chance she was hiding from a criminal past, she was nevertheless not being totally open and honest with him. Well, he'd soon put an end to that. First, he'd try to look on the internet using what he already knew. Then, tomorrow, when they were once again together for the entire day, he'd start asking Paige pointed questions. If she continued to be as evasive as she'd been so far, he'd know as much or more than if she aired her concerns.

Was it necessary to be that insistent? *Yes,* he answered easily. What she was hiding might play no part in this current investigation but it was coloring her responses to the point where he couldn't read her the way he did most folks. That made her unpredictable. And being unpredictable made her a lot harder to protect. He had to know more, to make sure nothing pertinent escaped him. He just had to.

Paige's sleep was fitful, shallow. The curtains over the motel window were so thick that they blocked out any light. That's why when Max nudged her with his cold, wet nose, she assumed it must be morning.

She yawned and stretched. "Hi, boy. Do you want to go out? Is that it?"

The dog's response was to race to the door then turn in tight circles.

Paige sighed as she swung her feet to the carpeted floor. "Okay. Hold your horses. I don't have a robe so you'll have to wait till I can get dressed."

It did occur to her to phone Cade's room to inform him she needed to walk Max but the thought of a few minutes' privacy and peace was terribly appealing. Nobody knew where she was staying, right? It shouldn't be dangerous to simply slip out and exercise her poor dog for a few minutes.

Crossing to the chair where she'd piled her clothing, she paused a moment to peek behind the heavy drapes. There was a faint glow in the eastern sky but it wasn't fully light out yet. Not that that mattered. After all, the motel surroundings were well lit and although the temperature would be chilly, it was only a few yards from her door to the grass where she'd be walking Max.

She slipped her clothes on and shoved her feet into

her sneakers. Once Max's needs were taken care of she'd have plenty of time to shower and maybe even wash and dry her hair.

Thinking about how relaxing the hot water would feel, especially on her achy shoulder, she pulled on her jacket, made sure she had the key card for her room, and snapped the leash on the excited dog. Seeing the way Max always greeted the day was invigorating. Often, Paige wished she had half his energy and even a quarter of his joy.

"Okay, now be quiet," Paige warned as she eased open the door. "We don't want to wake Cade."

Max was already whining and straining against the leash in his desire to reach the grass exercise strip.

She had to grin. "I know, I know. I'm hurrying."

In her haste she didn't realize how hard the door to her room would slam if she didn't keep hold of it. The resulting thud echoed along the exterior hallway and made her cringe.

Oops. Not good, she thought, pausing just long enough to put an ear to Cade's door. There was no sound of activity in his room. She'd gotten away with it. *Whew!*

Cade awoke with a start, unsure of what had disturbed him. Heart thumping, he sat up in bed and listened. Traffic on the street was little more than a hum and since the November weather was anything but balmy, his room air conditioner wasn't running to make background noise.

He looked at his watch. It was probably way too early to rouse Paige. However, since he was wide awake he decided to put the coffeemaker in the room to good use.

Better to have some caffeine in his system than greet her *before* coffee, the way he had previously.

That memory made him smile. Paige was an extraordinary person all right. Very few folks, men or women, could have faced all she had recently and remained so level-headed. No doubt it had helped that they'd been able to bring her big dog along but that alone wasn't enough to change a flighty female into someone as courageous in the face of danger as Paige was. Even when she was scared to death she was still able to act in her own defense. In her case, he wasn't sure whether that was an asset or a drawback.

He pulled on his western cut slacks while he waited for the coffee to brew, then poured himself a cup. He'd shave before calling Paige's room, he decided, just in case she was the kind of person who got ready to go in a hurry. It was probably almost light outside already.

Carrying the plastic cup of steaming coffee and taking cautious sips, Cade walked to the window and slipped his free hand between the sections of drapery to push them aside.

When he looked out and spotted Paige he choked. Coughed. Dribbled coffee down the side of the cup and burned his fingers. "What the…"

He jerked open his door. "Hey! What do you think you're doing?"

Instead of looking repentant, she merely waved and smiled.

Barefoot and without dress shirt or jacket, Cade hesitated to chase after her. He quickly surveyed the area and saw no immediate threat. Nevertheless, he thought better of continuing to shout and draw unwanted attention, so he motioned with his whole arm while nodding toward the hallway.

"Come on, come on," he murmured in disgust. "Get back here where you belong."

Paige turned away and concentrated on her dog rather than heed his orders. Cade was furious. She was going to force him to go fetch her.

He looked both ways to be sure the coast was clear, then stepped off the curb. The cement walkway had been only slightly colder than the asphalt he now felt beneath his bare feet but at least the halls had been swept clean. Pebbles of varying sizes and sharpness littered the parking lot. Half walking, half hobbling, he stormed toward her, determined to give her a piece of his mind that she'd never forget.

If he hadn't been so angry he might have noticed an approaching vehicle sooner. It was the sound of its powerful engine that first caught his attention. He glanced up, following the noise to its source.

The car was big. And black. And racing directly at him as if he were a deer caught in the crosshairs of a rifle scope.

Paige screamed at the same moment Cade realized he was in jeopardy.

He threw his coffee, dived between two parked cars and hit the ground rolling. A sharp pain cut through him near his ribs. Was he hit? Shot?

In seconds he realized that his only injuries were sore ribs and a few scrapes.

Cade gritted his teeth. He deserved far worse than that for leaving his room unarmed. Some guardian *he* was.

At this point, all he could think about was that it might be *her* lying there injured. That notion hurt more than his actual injuries.

ELEVEN

Time seemed to stop for Paige. Standing there with her hand pressed to the base of her throat she could barely breathe, barely move. Had the car actually hit Cade? Was it her fault that another innocent person had been injured—or worse?

Max pulled her toward the prone figure of the Ranger as the passing vehicle slued around a corner and roared away.

"Whoa, call him off," Cade ordered as he sat up.

"Are you okay?"

"Yeah, except for a few bruises and a lot of dog slobber." He levered himself to his feet. "Did you get the license number?"

"No, I never thought…" She could tell from his tight expression that her flimsy excuse was going to lead right into the lecture he was planning to deliver. Well, maybe she deserved it, although if he hadn't come outside when he did, everything might have been okay.

Paige held up her hand, palm out, to ward off the anticipated rebuke and realized then that she was shaking like a sapling in a Texas tornado. "You don't have to say it. I know I should have told you Max needed to go out but it was so early I thought it would be okay. I did check the parking lot. Honest, I did. There wasn't a soul out here."

"Yeah, so did I. They were probably watching from a distance," Cade said, looking perturbed. "It's not all your fault. I should have been armed." He nodded toward the rooms. "Come on. Let's get back inside before my toes freeze off."

"I really am sorry. I'm still not used to being some-body's target."

"*I* should be used to it," he said, starting to pick his way across the pavement as if his feet were sore. "I was positive I heard you promise not to leave your room without telling me."

"It was all Max's idea. He made me do it," Paige said, hoping a quip, no matter how silly, would help temper the Ranger's mood. He didn't smile but he did raise an eyebrow at her.

"Then I suppose I'll have to handcuff the *dog* instead of you."

"Lots of luck making that work." She chanced a smile. "His wrists are the same diameter as his paws."

They mounted the sidewalk and Paige glanced down. "Uh-oh. Look. Your foot is bleeding."

"It's nothing. I have a first aid kit in my truck."

"Then get it," she said. "The least I can do is bandage you up."

"Not on your life. If you think your neighbors are bad about gossip, you should hang around the folks *I* work with. I can just hear what Captain Parker would say if anybody reported that we'd been seen coming out of the same motel room after having spent time in there together. I'll take care of the cut myself."

Although she saw the wisdom in his statement she was nevertheless hurt. "You don't trust me?"

Cade snorted cynically. "Let's just say I know better than to let myself be put in a compromising position, no matter how innocent it really is. *Why* do you think I left the door open before?"

"Okay. Have it your way."

As Paige withdrew, unlocked her own room and entered, she was positive she heard him mutter something that sounded an awful lot like, "It's me I don't trust."

That couldn't have been what he'd actually said. Of course it couldn't. He'd never given her the slightest reason to distrust him, nor had he made any inappropriate advances.

Well, unless she counted the way he'd hugged her after her flat tire and narrow escape on the side of the highway. She grew thoughtful, then decided that if Cade had wanted to embrace her for personal reasons, he'd missed several more excellent opportunities. *Like when my overnight bag was stolen, not to mention a few moments ago.*

No, she concluded. Cade hadn't been making a pass at her before and he certainly hadn't meant anything like that just now. They were professional colleagues, that was all. *Bummer.*

Paige looked down at her dog and smiled. "Max, old boy, I am officially a doofus. Do you know that?"

When Max wiggled his back end and looked up at her as if he was smiling, she threw her arms around his neck and hugged him tightly. What a sweetie! If people were half as easy for her to understand as animals were, she'd feel a lot more well-adjusted.

And probably a lot less lonely, she added ruefully. Funny. Until very recently she'd been positive that she was fully content with her job and an uncomplicated routine. Now, suddenly, she was beginning to wish there were more people in her life.

Paige huffed. Who was she kidding? She didn't need big groups of friends to make her feel accepted. All she needed was one person. The one who had assured her that she was dressed well enough to visit the governor no matter what she happened to be wearing. The one currently occupying the adjoining room.

By the time Cade had treated the small cut on his foot and had finished shaving and dressing, his stomach was growling like a bear just coming out of hibernation. A big ranch-style Texas breakfast was what he needed. He made a face at himself in the bathroom mirror as he combed his hair. The only way he was going to convince Paige to visit a restaurant with him was to find one that would welcome Max. Chances of that were slim to none. Unless…

He slung his belt around his waist, adjusted the holster placement, then pulled on his jacket before ducking outside to knock on her door.

When she greeted him she was obviously ready to leave. He eyed her from head to toe. "Nice choice. I like that new sweater."

"Thanks. When I saw this shade of green I couldn't pass it up. You don't think it's too fancy?"

Cade shook his head. "Of course not. The sparkles really look good." *Especially with the beautiful green color of your eyes.*

"Well, I'm ready. Just let me grab my purse."

"Okay. Listen, I was thinking. If the techs in San Antonio say they can do some of the work for you, why don't we take a run down there today?"

"I have way too much to do in my office. I can't waste time being away."

"It's not a waste if it lets you get started on the modeling sooner. Didn't your supplier tell you it might be weeks before he could ship you a new laser scanner?"

"Yes, but..."

"Then why fight it? You and I both want the same thing. Besides, the drive will give us a chance to relax for a change."

"Assuming the bad guys don't catch us sneaking out of town?"

"Yeah. Something like that. We could probably find a restaurant along the way and get a decent meal instead of eating on the truck tailgate again and half freezing to death."

"I suppose I could call ahead and see if their lab's equipment is in use. I could also find out if it's detailed enough for STL—stereo lithography."

"I've heard of that. Isn't that where a computer lays down one thin layer of resin powder at a time and then fuses it?"

"Yes. The process is called SLS, selective laser sintering. The technique was developed for making prototype models for industry but it's perfect for forensics, too."

"How long does it take?"

"Usually several days from the scan to the finished model, but if they've already made a usable scan of the skeleton, they should be able to use that and go right to work."

"Okay. Call them and see. Maybe they can start on it early and we can pick it up later today."

"We, Kemosabe?" Paige was grinning.

"Of course, *we*. I'm not about to leave you and I figured you'd insist on being there to watch."

"Smart man."

"I'm glad you admit it." He was pleased to see her spirits lifting as they planned their next move. "Tell you what. If we have to wait for the lab in San Antonio to finish, why don't we visit the crime scene where the skull was found? That's down there, too."

"Thanks, but no thanks. If we *do* go, I'll be staying with the technicians to supervise. And speaking of the skull, we'll need to stop at my office and get it out of the safe."

"Okay. Make your call and let's either hit the road or find something else constructive to do here."

As he waited and listened to her speaking with the lab techs on the phone, he realized he had another reason for wanting to take Paige to San Antonio. The trip might give him a chance to show off his ranch, even if all they did was drive past it.

Why? Because that spread was his pride and joy and impressing her had suddenly become important. There was no use trying to deny it so he didn't. He cared what she thought of him and of his home. That was all there was to it.

"Yeah, right," he muttered, thoroughly disgusted with

himself. The mere sight of her was starting to affect him strangely, as if he were a little country boy getting a glimpse of his first pony or his first BB gun.

That thought made Cade grin and laugh out loud just as she hung up the phone.

"What's so funny?" Paige asked.

"I am." He indicated the telephone she'd been using. "So, are we going?"

"Yes. Their equipment isn't as new as mine was but they have the time to build the replica. My only other choice would be to use the actual bone for a base and I've been asked not to do that this time."

"Come on, then. Let's go pick up the skull in case we might need it and hit the road."

"You're not going to tell me what was so funny just now?"

"Nope. Maybe later."

"Promise?"

He laughed again. "No. I know better than to do that, especially in view of the way you feel about making promises."

Cade was checking the parking area for safety as he escorted her toward his truck. He helped her and Max in, watching as she scooted over all the way to the other door. To his relief she was still smiling. That was a good sign. By the time they'd reached the San Antonio area, maybe she'd have relaxed enough to tell him a little something more about herself.

It wasn't enough for him to have learned of her sister's kidnapping from his father. He wanted Paige to tell him. To trust him enough to open up and let him into a portion of her life that she'd been guarding so well that no one she worked with seemed to be aware of it.

Sliding behind the wheel he started the truck, then turned to her. "Before we go, I want you to know I wasn't blaming you for what happened this morning when I mentioned keeping promises."

She lowered her gaze and started staring at her clasped hands in her lap. "I shouldn't have gone out alone."

"No, you shouldn't have. But just because a similar vehicle caused problems before, that doesn't mean this was the same one. Or that the driver was really after you."

She looked up, eyes shining. "Actually, it looked like it was trying to run *you* down this time, not me."

Nodding, Cade checked his mirrors before backing out and heading for the main highway. "That is a possibility."

His hands gripped the wheel tightly. In his opinion, it was far *more* likely that the criminals responsible were trying to get rid of him only to clear a path to Paige. That must never happen.

Clenching his jaw, he realized that he'd already made a grave mistake. He'd let himself begin to care for her. And that emotional involvement would cloud his insight, whether he wanted it to or not.

The Ranger's Company D headquarters in San Antonio sat at the Y of two roads. Housing developments were beginning to encroach on the east and southwest. To the north lay undeveloped farmland. Unlike Austin, there were few trees around these buildings and even less shrubbery.

That suited Paige fine. The less places there were for their adversaries to hide in ambush, the better she liked it.

When Cade parked in the employee lot, Paige saw plenty of spaces that would accommodate the full length of a truck and stock trailer. Even in big cities like Austin, there might be need for a mounted patrol and Rangers dearly loved hauling their horses around with them whenever possible.

She began to scoot past the steering wheel while Max attempted to squeeze through next to the gas and brake pedals.

Cade grabbed the trailing end of the leash. He was having trouble keeping a straight face. "Okay. You can bring the dog."

"Thanks. Don't worry. Max is housebroken."

"That was a real relief to see when we went to the governor's office. I must confess I was a little worried about him."

"Who? The governor or Max?" She giggled.

All Cade did in reply was roll his eyes and shake his head as he held the door for her. "You are a strange and interesting woman, Miss Paige."

"Thanks, I think."

"You're welcome. Let's stop by the office. I'll introduce you."

"Actually, I was here not too long ago," she said pleasantly. "I drove down to make the sketches for Corinna Pike, remember?"

She'd also met Captain Pike before his murder and although she hadn't known him well, she could tell by the unusually subdued atmosphere when they entered the building that he was still sorely missed.

Cade led the way into one of the private offices. A tall, sandy-haired Ranger rose politely from the chair behind his desk. Paige recognized him as Captain Benjamin Fritz, the officer who had taken Pike's place after his untimely death.

While Cade briefly filled Fritz in about the vandalism of her studio, Paige offered her hand and shook his.

"Good to see you again, ma'am," the captain said. "Sorry to hear about your troubles. Hopefully, you'll enjoy a peaceful visit to our city."

"Thanks. If it's quieter than Austin's been lately, I know I will." Paige stepped back. "I actually came to use your lab. They tell me they may be able to help with my work."

"Good," Fritz said. "Y'all just make yourselves at home." He cast a warning glance at Cade. "See that you keep this lady safe. She's a very valuable asset to the Texas Rangers."

"Yes, sir." Cade touched the brim of his white hat in a parting salute.

"Maybe we shouldn't have stopped here before going to the lab," Paige said quietly as they left. "Your boss sounded a little put out."

"Don't worry about it. I'll have to file a stack of reports and the captain would have learned all the gory details then, anyway." He huffed. "I'm getting so far behind in my paperwork since I started hanging around with you, I may not catch up till spring—if then."

"Hey, it's not my fault."

"I know. I wasn't blaming you." He took her elbow

to guide her through the front of the building, crossing the narrow, grassy, open area that was tucked between two sections that formed a U shape. The stars and stripes was displayed there, just above the red-white-and-blue Texas state flag with its one, enormous star.

Sunlight on the fluttering banners made them seem almost alive, as if they were proud to represent state and nation. Paige smiled to herself. She was proud to do so, too. This was her destiny. She gave new life to the lost and helped bring justice where otherwise there might be none.

When she'd first gone to work as a forensic artist she'd kept track of every success, counting each like a trophy. Now that almost five years had passed, however, she'd lost track. That was okay. She didn't need to cite numbers to know that her work was critical to the success of law enforcement, the Rangers in particular.

Cade held the door for her and she passed through into the forensics division.

"Hey, you can't bring that dog in here," someone hollered.

Instead of leaving, Paige passed the leash to Cade and relieved him of the padded case. "Do you mind?"

"Nope. We'll wait outside."

"Good. I don't know how long this will take but it won't be fast. Make yourselves comfortable."

She had to smile while she watched both Cade and Max amble over to an elm that was casting little shade at this time of the year. Man and dog looked equally disappointed, right down to their hang-dog expressions and plodding steps.

Continuing to grin, Paige focused her attention on

the gangly, sandy-haired, freckled young man who had shouted at her. His ID badge said his name was Lonnie and he looked barely old enough to be out of high school, let alone in charge of anything in a forensics lab.

"Sorry about that, Lonnie. I wasn't thinking. I'm Paige Bryant, from Austin. I called this morning and talked to James. He said you'd be able to build a sinter copy for me. Is he here?"

"I'll go check. You got some ID?"

She reached into her purse for her wallet and displayed her driver's license as well as her Texas Ranger Associate card. "See? It's really me."

"Yeah, well, maybe. You did come in with a Ranger so I guess you're legit. I don't wanna get into more trouble over stupid skulls."

"Trouble?"

He rolled his eyes and arched his brows beneath tousled hair that had fallen across part of his forehead. "Oh, yeah. You don't know what trouble is till you almost hand evidence like that to the wrong guy."

Paige's heart was in her throat. "What happened? When? How?"

"It was just this morning. Boy, was James steamed when he found out I almost got fooled. Good thing for me the guy was so jumpy. He ran off when I asked for an ID."

"He didn't get away with anything?"

"Nope. Must have been on a scavenger hunt or something dumb like that. Hang on. I'll go get the boss."

Still fighting the panic she'd felt when the technician had made his confession, Paige stuck her head out the door to let Cade know what was going on.

"Keep your eyes open," she called. "There was somebody here earlier who tried to pick up evidence that didn't belong to him." She shuddered. "I can't imagine what we'd have done if they'd handed over *our* skull, even if they do have the data already stored."

"Could it have been a mistake?"

"Not the way the kid inside tells it," Paige said soberly. "It's a good thing we stopped for breakfast. Whoever is trying to interfere probably thought we'd already gotten here."

A sober nod was Cade's only reply. Paige could see his gaze moving over their surroundings as though he were a sentry on guard duty in the middle of a war zone.

"I guess they haven't given up."

"Well, they're going about it so stupidly that it's almost laughable. Nothing is going to stop me. Period."

Seeing the way Cade's shoulders tensed and his back grew ramrod straight, she knew where his thoughts had carried him. He'd been present during most of her trials. Yes, she was uneasy but she was also fighting mad. She would work 24/7 to get this face reconstructed if need be.

And in the meantime, as soon as she was back at her own repaired computer, she was going to run the programs that showed probable features, using 3-D scans of the bone structure, and circulate that picture, as well. They were going to solve this case. *She* was going to solve this case. Or die trying.

TWELVE

Cade notified his fellow Rangers as well as the State Troopers about the stranger's efforts to pick up evidence, suggested they check surveillance tapes, then settled down under the tree again. He scratched Max's ears and was rewarded with a noisy sigh. "Glad you appreciate me," Cade said. "I'd heard that making friends with a woman's pet was the sure way to impress her. I'm sure glad you're not a cat. 'Course, I could always stuff a cat into a carrying case. That would be pretty hard to do with an animal as big as you."

That silly image brought a chuckle. "And here I am, cooling my heels and talking to a dog."

Laughter from behind him caused him to tense. He whirled and tilted back his hat to see who was there.

"Daniel. Don't sneak up on me like that," Cade said to the closest person, noting that there were three Rangers in the group: Oliver Drew, Daniel Boone Riley and Gisella Hernandez.

The men remained standing, apparently highly amused by the ramblings they'd overheard, while Gisella knelt and began to make a fuss over Max.

"I'd always heard that walking a dog was the perfect

way to attract women," Daniel said, nodding toward the dark-haired female Ranger. "Guess it's so."

Gisella's brown eyes narrowed as she gave her comrades a derisive look. "Knock it off, boys, or I'll have to report you."

"She wouldn't dare," Oliver Drew argued. "She knows there are too many of us to take on all at once. We'd make her life miserable."

Cade was about to speak in her defense when Daniel did it for him. "I'm sure she had to work twice as hard as you did, Drew, or she wouldn't have gotten this far."

"Yeah, yeah." Stuffing his hands in his pockets the antagonist sauntered away.

"What's his problem?" Cade asked.

"You know Oliver." Daniel shrugged and smiled. "So, since Max is here, I assume Paige can't be far away."

"She's using the lab."

"And you're sitting out here? That's a surprise. I thought you two were like Siamese twins."

Cade eyed the dog. "He was banished so I had no choice. If anything happened to him, Paige would never forgive me."

Gisella's eyebrows arched as she glanced over. "Well, well. Do I detect a little romance in the air?"

He gave her a harsh look of warning, hoping that would suffice. It didn't. She began to smile so he simply said, "No comment."

Softening, she studied him. "I'm glad. It's about time you settled down the way Anderson and Fritz have."

"Uh-oh," Daniel said. "Maybe it's catching like a virus." He backed away, hands raised in front of him as if fending off an invisible attack. "Just see that you don't give it to me. Once was enough."

"How is your son these days?" Cade asked.

"He's a typical teen. Unfortunately."

Gisella got to her feet, much to the dog's apparent disappointment. She chuckled as she looked down. "Give me a faithful dog or horse anytime. They're too dumb to be devious."

"Which is why you don't find many of those critters doing hard time," Cade joked, "although Paige did tell me she rescued Max from the pound so I guess you could say he'd been in jail."

"Poor guy. Well, I suppose I'd better get back to my desk." She gave Daniel and Cade an exaggerated look of disdain. "Some of us have work to do. See you later."

"Yeah," Cade said, rising. "I think I'll grab my laptop from the truck. Might as well work out here while I'm waiting."

Daniel fell into step beside him as Cade started off. "So, what's the latest on Paige's truck? Was it a bullet hole in her tire?"

"Yes. If you see her, don't bring it up, okay? She's stopped asking when she'll get the truck back and I'd just as soon keep driving her around myself. It's safer."

"And a lot more fun," Daniel countered, grinning. "I hate to agree with Gisella but I think you've caught the bug, buddy." He sobered. "What does Paige think?"

Cade sighed. "Beats me. She's so engrossed in her work it's hard to get her to talk about anything else, let alone discuss her feelings." Reaching the edge of the parking lot he paused. "That was one of the reasons I encouraged her to make this trip. I was hoping it would give us a chance to have a casual conversation while I drove."

"Did it?"

"Not so far. Not even when we stopped at a roadside diner for a quick breakfast. But I have high hopes for the return trip. I think Paige will settle down once she has everything she needs to begin recreating the face in clay."

Daniel extended his hand and they shook as they parted. "Well, hang in there. Whatever happens between you and Paige, remember, her reconstruction has to come first."

Deep inside Cade lay the urge to disagree, yet he knew his fellow Ranger was right. Their work took precedence. When had he lost sight of that?

The answer was easy. The instant he'd let himself care too much. He'd tried to turn away from Paige, to resist her, but circumstances had kept conspiring to draw them together until his heart was so involved in her life he had no choice.

Although he'd tried, over and over, to convince himself the change was merely the result of their current case, he knew better. He was deeply, irrevocably in love with her. There had been times, such as the instance when he'd come to her rescue beside the highway, he'd actually thought she was beginning to return his growing affection. They were certainly getting along better in many ways.

Yet she was still holding a part of herself back, still refusing to open up to him the way he thought she should if she truly was interested in an emotional commitment with him.

Cade supposed she'd come around in her own time. The trouble was, as soon as she completed this job for the Rangers, he'd be out of excuses to remain at her side. Once that happened, he didn't know how he was going to be able to just walk away without knowing her mind-set. Not only would he be constantly worried about her, it would practically kill him if he ever learned she'd fallen in love with someone else in his absence.

The thought alone was enough to make him feel as if a pile of rocks the size of the entire Texas panhandle was sitting smack-dab in the middle of his stomach—never mind the twist the notion was giving to his heart.

Paige knew she was making a nuisance of herself but she couldn't help it. The lab in San Antonio was so primitive in contrast to the equipment she'd had in Austin it was driving her crazy.

She'd been satisfied by her observations so far, although she still intended to make precise measurements of the reproduction later to check for accuracy. Beyond that, there was little she could do other than pace or lean over the system that was painstakingly building the copy out of powder, minute layer by minute layer.

Finally, she decided she'd be of more use to herself and to everyone else if she didn't cause a headache by concentrating too hard. Excusing herself—much to the others' obvious relief—she ventured out to see what Cade was up to.

The Ranger had his back propped against a tree, legs folded, and was concentrating on the screen of his laptop.

Paige saw him look up, smile and close the lid on the

computer. She inclined her head toward it. "Hey, don't stop working on my account."

"I was just surfing the web. Got all my reports done and emailed already."

"Good for you."

When he patted the ground beside him she plopped onto the grass and began massaging her stiff neck muscles until Max interrupted by trying to climb into her lap.

"Down, boy. Sit," Cade ordered firmly.

To Paige's astonishment, the dog stepped back politely and obeyed. "Wow, I'm impressed. I guess you guys have bonded, huh?"

"Guess so. Is the lab work finished?"

"No. I just needed a break. Standing there while that carriage runs back and forth is like watching paint dry."

"A little boring?"

"You could say that."

"How much longer will it be?"

"I don't know. I'm guessing—hoping—only an hour or so more."

"Okay. Then we'll wait, unless you're starving. I was going to suggest we go grab a bite to eat before we start back for Austin."

"I liked that little Mom and Pop place where we had breakfast this morning," Paige said. "It felt safe."

"The food was good, too."

"I agree." Exercising her neck she leaned her head back, then began making slow circles and shrugging her shoulders.

"Turn around," Cade said.

Guessing why and choosing not to ask in case he might change his mind, Paige scooted sideways slightly and lifted her long hair.

The moment Cade's fingers began to gently tighten on the knotted neck muscles beneath her jacket, she sighed. "Right there. Now a little to the left. Mmmm."

"You're so tense I don't know how you can stand it," he commented, continuing the massage. "Are you always this tied up?"

"Not all the time. I do have my moments, though. Especially when I'm involved in this kind of work and we have a deadline."

"That's not exactly true," Cade said.

"It is for me. I always operate under a tight, self-imposed schedule even if I haven't been given a real one. Every day a victim remains unidentified is one more day their family has to wonder."

"You understand that very well, don't you?"

She scowled and turned to look at him. "Why would you think that?"

"Maybe because of what happened to your sister when you were ten years old."

Wishing that he wasn't looking at her with such clear empathy, she bristled. "How much do you already know?"

"Enough. My dad was a State Trooper at the time of the kidnapping, and I was able to look up some additional details." He cleared his throat. "Dad was one of the men assigned to search for your little sister. Being a teenager, I didn't pay attention to most of his cases but the more I think about it, the more I remember how upset he was that they weren't able to make any headway."

"So was I."

"Of course you were. I saw my dad fly into a rage and throw things when he got so frustrated over their failure. That was rare for him. He was usually even-tempered and kept his cool, no matter what. But not back then."

"I'm sorry. I wish…"

"Hey, don't be *sorry*."

Cade reached for her hand and she let him hold it. Truth to tell, she was so conflicted she didn't know which way to turn. In desperate need of moral support, she was also furious at him for prying into her past. She let her misty gaze meet his and was astounded at how touched, how sympathetic he appeared to be. She opened her mouth with the intent of arguing. No words came.

"Nothing that happened, then or later, was your fault," he told her.

Paige found her voice. "That's not what my parents said."

"They were frantic. Stressed. At a loss and feeling totally helpless, which is exactly what you were feeling, too. It's hardly surprising that they didn't know how to act. News reports said your father nearly took apart the police station on one of his many visits."

"Really?"

"Yes. Really. You know, only God can help you handle the rough stuff like what your family went through. It doesn't matter how your parents acted then, or even how they behave now. What counts is your relationship with the good Lord."

"God gave up on me long ago," she whispered.

To her relief, Cade didn't pressure her or preach anymore. He did, however, pull her into his embrace and hold her close for a brief moment. That was enough to cause a wayward tear to slip past her lashes and slide down one cheek.

Paige wasn't touched so much by the fact that he was hugging her as she was by the reason behind it. He knew she was hurting. He cared. And he didn't blame her. That was the biggest surprise. After all this time, after all her weeping and wailing and self-reproach, she had finally found solace.

At that precious moment she almost took his advice, turned back to God and gave thanks through prayer. Her heart wanted to. It was her mind that held her back.

Giving Paige time to compose herself, Cade opened his laptop again and checked his email to see if everything was still peaceful in Austin. It was. And since he'd been sitting out there with Max, nothing odd had occurred locally, either.

He smiled when he noticed Paige's quizzical expression. "Looks good all around. No more problems reported. The sheriff hasn't seen anybody messing with your house, either."

"That's good news. I still think it's too soon to tell Angela she can go home, though. Don't you?"

"Yes. Let's wrap up this case first and then talk about that."

"Which reminds me. I need to go see how close the lab is to being done." She gracefully got to her feet. "Don't go away."

Cade nodded. "Not a chance. I'll be ready to roll whenever you are."

He knew Paige well enough to tell that it was a

struggle for her to smile and act so nonchalant. That was all right. Now that she knew he was fully aware of her tragic past, he figured she'd eventually get around to discussing it. At least he hoped so. She needed to unburden herself as well as study the details of the case as an adult so she could stop viewing the loss from a child's perspective.

If freeing her of that undeserved guilt brought her happiness, all the better. In the meantime, he was going to continue praying that she'd recognize the emotional freedom that was available if only she'd exercise her Christian faith instead of denying it.

Cade's jaw clenched. Not even a man who loved her the way he did could make that kind of decision for her. All he could do was wait and pray and try to protect her while she sorted it all out.

Closing his eyes, he prayed silently for the strength and wisdom he'd need.

When he opened them again, Paige was coming toward him carrying not one bag, but two. And this time her grin was genuine.

She held them up, one in each hand. "Got 'em. Let's hit the road."

THIRTEEN

The drive back to Austin seemed unusually long. Paige had been daydreaming so much she almost missed pointing out the café where she'd told Cade she wanted to stop.

"Look! There it is. Pull in."

"You sure that's where you want to eat?"

"Positive. You haven't seen any sign that we're being followed, have you?"

"Nope, not a thing."

"Then it should be safe to lock everything in the truck with Max, give him some ventilation and go in to eat like we did this morning. Right?"

"Sure. As long as I can find a parking place right outside a window. We'll want to keep a close eye on everything, the same way we did the last time."

"Perfect." Paige pointed. "There's an empty spot!"

"You must be really hungry," he teased. "Can't say I blame you. We haven't eaten since breakfast."

Sliding out, Cade once again held the door while Paige shinnied across the seat to join him. This time, she'd held up her hand and ordered, "Stay" before the dog had had a chance to get the notion he was going with them.

"Poor old Max," Cade said as he shut and locked the door.

"Don't be fooled by that sad expression. He's very good at manipulating people by pretending he's miserable when he's not. It works on me almost every time."

She cast a backward glance at the truck as they entered the café and saw that the dog was circling in preparation for lying down on the passenger seat. With the real skull and the reproduction securely boxed and stored on the floor, she saw no problems. Besides, she added, slipping her hand into her pocket and feeling the disk containing the information from the 3-D scan, there was no way anybody was going to stop her now.

Cade's cell phone rang during their meal. He answered, nodded as he listened quietly, then thanked the caller and bid him goodbye.

"So, what else have our jungle friends been up to lately? I can hardly wait to hear."

"Who?"

She leaned across the table and cupped a hand around her mouth to say, "The Lions of Texas, silly."

"The call wasn't about them," he assured her. "I do wish you'd be more serious, Paige. This is not a game. These guys play for keeps."

"What can they do to me that's worse than watching some lowlife make off with my baby sister and having to accept everyone's opinion that she's long dead and it's all my fault? Huh?" Pushing herself back against the booth she crossed her arms and stared, chin up and her head cocked to one side, as if daring him to argue.

"*You* could be killed," Cade said, surprised to hear the rasp in his voice.

"I have no intention of getting killed," Paige said firmly. "I have you to protect me. And I should be done with the reconstruction in no time. After that, I can't see this threat continuing, can you?"

Cade didn't know whether to level with her or not. He decided it was better to alarm her than to let her become too complacent.

"Maybe. Maybe not," he said. "Organizations like the Lions don't get powerful by letting their enemies just ride off into the sunset and live happily ever after. They may still target you."

"Why? I'd be no threat then."

"I didn't say it made sense. I'm just saying that they're probably more ruthless than you can imagine."

"And the Texas Rangers are the best in the country, if not the whole world. You'll break up that drug ring soon and I plan to help you do it," She began to smile. "So, what's our next move, partner?"

He had to chuckle. "*Our* next move? I don't believe you. Aren't you at least a little scared?"

Nodding, she rolled her eyes. "There are times when I'm petrified, especially if I'm trapped in the dark like I was when you first came to see me, or about to be run down by a speeding car, or whatever. Then I think about Captain Pike and that poor man whose face I'm about to reconstruct and I get really mad. If I curl up in a corner and hide because I'm frightened, the bad guys win. I can't let that happen any more than you'd be willing to lay down your guns and quit pursuing justice."

"Bravo!" Cade said.

Paige giggled and blushed. "You need to brush up on your Spanish, cowboy. You should have said, 'Brava', with an *a*."

"Only if I'm calling you courageous. Besides, a cheer is a cheer," he countered. "In case I haven't told you this before, it's a great pleasure to be working with you."

"Back atcha," Paige quipped. She eyed his nearly empty plate. "Are you going to eat those fries? Because if you're not, I'd like to take them out to Max. He loves 'em with ketchup."

"Okay. I imagine it will be pretty messy but have at it," he said, passing the remnants of his dinner to her. "He'll be drooling on *your* knees this time, not mine. I'll go pay the bill, get you a takeout box and be right back."

"Okey-dokey."

At the counter he accepted his change, dropped the loose coins into a charity contribution container, then returned to the table with the empty plastic carton.

His jaw dropped. Paige's purse was still there but she wasn't.

Whirling, Cade scanned the quiet café. There was no sign of her. Could she have gone to use the ladies' room? Surely not without telling him. His jaw clamped, teeth gritting. If that woman was up to her old tricks of wandering off, he was going to give her a lecture she'd never forget.

And if she hadn't left of her own accord? His hands fisted. His heart lodged in his constricted throat. If someone had taken Paige from right under his nose, he'd never forgive himself.

She had stood to stretch while Cade was away from the table. Pausing next to the booth, she'd glanced casually out the window at the Ranger's white pickup for the hundredth time. Her jaw had dropped. *Oh, no!*

Paige was moving toward the door before she even thought about what she was doing. Some skinny kid in a backwards ball cap was trying to break into Cade's truck!

Dodging between the small tables and chairs she straight-armed the exit and burst through. It slammed behind her. She paid it no mind. Nothing mattered but getting to the truck before the car thief managed to open the door.

"Stop!" Paige shouted, closing the distance between herself and the truck. "Get away from there. Thief! Robber!" Her voice was shrill and she was attracting plenty of attention, as she'd intended, but no bystanders were making any moves to come to her aid.

She tackled the astonished car thief by grabbing his bony shoulder from behind and pushing him to the side. He wasn't hefty but he was wiry enough that he kept his balance. Still grasping the thin metal lever that he'd been using to try to open the locked door, he went into a crouch as if he might be preparing to attack.

Inside the truck, Max began growling, barking and clawing frantically at the window they'd left slightly open for ventilation.

Paige's first thought was for Max's welfare if the glass broke. Her second was that Cade was going to be livid about any more damage to his precious truck. Well, too bad. A window could be replaced. Living things could not.

Behind Paige, a woman screamed. She didn't look to see why because she'd have had to take her eyes off the thief to do so and she still wasn't sure whether he was going to make a run for it or attack. Judging by the feral look in his narrowed eyes, he wasn't sure, either.

Then he straightened, lifted the lever and took a menacing step toward her!

The bang of a gunshot was so loud, so close, it hurt Paige's senses and left her momentarily stunned.

She ducked and covered her ears with her hands. In the millisecond before she peeked out at the thief, he had turned tail and was scrambling across the crowded parking lot, half on all-fours, half running as if he expected the next bullet to catch up to him.

Someone grabbed Paige's arm. She screamed.

Cade had heard the restaurant's door slam at about the same time he'd discovered that Paige was missing. He'd wheeled and run outside just in time to see her tackling a slim, canvas-jacketed youth wearing a dirty baseball cap.

Pulling his .45, Cade had shouted, "Freeze!" The guy had lunged toward her instead of stopping, so Cade had fired a warning shot into the air.

Her adversary lit out, pretty much as expected, and disappeared among the many cars in the dirt parking lot next to the diner.

Cade reached for Paige, grasping her arm to pull her

erect. She began to screech and thrash like a coyote caught in the jaws of a pelt hunter's trap.

"Easy. It's me," Cade said, holstering his sidearm so he could draw her into his arms. "I've got you. You're safe now. He's gone."

Shuddering, she pressed her cheek to Cade's chest and slipped both arms around his waist. "I saw him trying to steal your truck."

"Maybe it wasn't the truck he wanted," Cade said, tensing and scanning the innocuous-looking parking lot. They'd begun to gather a crowd, particularly now that the passersby had seen that a Texas Ranger was involved and had deduced that the danger was over.

Eyes wide, Paige looked up at him. "The evidence, you mean?"

"Yes. We should have taken all that inside with us."

"But, we can easily have everything duplicated now that I have it on disk. Surely, they'd know that."

"That's true. Maybe all that guy wanted was a nice pickup."

Paige managed a wry chuckle. "With a big, ugly crease down one side and a barking dog inside it? Yeah, right. Max may be a wimp at heart but he didn't look it just now."

"Make up your mind. Do you want me to agree with you or not?" Cade kept an arm around her shoulders and started to guide her away. "Let's go back inside for a few minutes so we're out of sight while I phone in a report, take names of witnesses and notify the local sheriff. There'll have to be an internal investigation because I fired my weapon."

"Were you shooting at that man?"

"No. I'd never do that unless he posed a direct threat. I couldn't see if he had a gun or a knife. I wouldn't have shot him unless I was sure he was dangerous."

"All I saw was one of those thin metal bars that thieves use to break into locked vehicles. The way he was holding it after I pushed him away, it looked like he was going to take a swing at me."

"A slim-jim, you mean? I saw it, too. I'll have the sheriff's men scour the parking lot in case he dropped it. Fingerprints would be nice. I'd like to have something we can enter into IAFIS, the Integrated Automated Fingerprint Identification System, and see what we come up with."

"Right now, about all I want to do is get my dog and find a place to sit down. I was afraid Max was going to break the side window of the truck trying to get out."

"Okay. Just keep a tight hold on the leash in case he spots the thief again."

"Right."

She'd left one arm around Cade's waist in spite of his gun and the other gear on his belt, and was sticking to him like glue. That felt so right it made his heart race and his breathing grow shallow, uneven. At this point he didn't care what anyone else thought or said. He was staying as close to Paige as she'd allow and he didn't care who noticed.

Paige wondered how much longer they were going to have to delay before resuming their trip. She hadn't realized how exhausted she was until the furor had died down and she'd lost the surge of adrenaline that had been powering her ever since she'd gone to Max's defense.

She felt a bit sorry for Cade, having to explain his actions, but there was no way she could help him other than to stay out of his way and keep quiet. Doing so was usually a trial for her, especially since she liked being involved in ongoing investigations.

"This time, I'm just a tad *too* involved if you ask me," she muttered, talking to the weary dog that lay at her feet. She sighed deeply. It became a yawn before she was finished and she covered her mouth.

"Tired?" Cade joined her on the secluded bench beside the restaurant's side door and handed her the purse she'd left in the booth inside.

"Yes. How's it going?"

"Fine, considering."

"Are you in trouble for shooting?"

"I don't think so, at least nobody's said so yet." He held out a hand. "Come on, let's hit the road again."

"We're done here?"

He nodded. "I dusted the door of my truck and managed to lift a few partial prints. They may pan out, they may not. Nobody was able to come up with the guy's tool so what I got is all we have."

"I didn't see a black SUV this time, did you?"

"No. I suspect they've changed vehicles now that we've gotten pictures from several surveillance cameras."

"I thought you said their license plate was stolen?"

"It was. But we do have some long-distance photos of the driver. They're being checked at my office till you get your systems back up and running. Then they'll email them to you."

Paige sighed again. "Shouldn't be long. I was promised that computer ASAP."

"Can't rush things like that," Cade said. "We don't want to lose the data you already had stored and have to start over."

"Goodness, no." Paige almost gasped. "It took me months to load and process that the first time."

"See? All in good time."

When he started to walk, Paige boldly slipped her hand into his and was thrilled when his fingers closed around hers. His hand was warm. Large and comforting. Yet his grip was as gentle as a caress.

She'd had boyfriends in high school and had dated a little after that, particularly in tech school when she'd taken the special courses that had qualified her for her current job. But never had she felt this kind of true belonging, this peaceful presence that bathed her heart in joy and left her yearning for more.

Her feelings didn't make sense. They didn't have to. Not now. Later, when the danger and excitement were over and she and Cade were back to their regular assignments, then she'd analyze what seemed to be happening between them.

She tightened her grip and felt him return the soothing pressure. Her fingers tingled. Her eyes grew moist. Her loneliness had vanished.

Paige blinked to help clear her head. *That* was the other thing that was so different! Someone was beside her because he wanted to be. Someone cared. For her. Just for her. And that sensation was so uncommon it took her breath away and made her go weak in the knees.

"Are you all right?" Cade asked.

His deep voice rippled along her spine and tickled the fine hairs at the nape of her neck. It was almost too much sensory input, yet too important to miss. Every moment was precious. Every word the Ranger spoke went straight to her heart and found a home there.

"Paige?" he prodded.

When she looked up at him he was smiling as if enjoying a good joke. "What?"

Cade chuckled. "Nothing. You were daydreaming again. I've been told that's a sign of genius."

"Then I must be the smartest woman in Texas," she said sheepishly, "because I'm always getting lost in my thoughts."

"At least they looked like they were good this time," Cade said. "You were smiling."

High color rose to warm her cheeks. "Was I?"

"Uh-huh. Care to tell me what you were thinking about?"

Paige shook her head and stared down at Max rather than let her expression reveal too much. She forced a sharp laugh. "Nope. I don't think that's a good idea."

"Why not?"

Feeling his hold tighten around her hand she sensed that he was guessing far too correctly so she eased her fingers from between his and used them to double her hold on the dog's leash.

Finally, she decided that Cade deserved an answer so she said, "Because Texas Rangers are already too full of themselves. If I told you how much I appreciate all you've done for me, your head might get so big your cowboy hat wouldn't fit anymore."

Cade was still laughing softly—and Paige's cheeks were still flushed—when they climbed back into the truck and resumed their trip north to Austin.

She sneaked sidelong glances at him as he drove. Every look brought a new surge of jubilation. She already knew each smile line on his handsome face by heart and the more she studied him, the more she knew she was deeply, hopelessly in love.

Cade Jarvis was not simply a good Ranger and a nice man, he was her personal hero, no matter how foolish that sounded. She might never tell him so, of course, but she was through denying the truth to herself.

FOURTEEN

Cade didn't relax his guard in the days that followed, not even after the attacks on Paige and her surroundings abruptly ceased. Experience had taught him that just because a threat seemed neutralized there was no guarantee that it wouldn't reappear later, perhaps in some other form.

Paige had booted up her repaired and refurbished PC and had sounded delighted with its new speed. She wasn't, however, nearly as pleased with him as the days crept by.

"Stop pacing, will you? You're making me nervous."

"Sorry." Cade approached her desk. "What are you doing now?"

"Making a two-dimensional rendering. I needed a short break from working with the clay."

"How does this kind of thing work?" He peered at her computer monitor and saw a rotating image of the original skull with pegs sticking out all over it. "That looks like what you did to it before you started adding the clay."

"It is," Paige said. "This technique was developed by

one of my famous predecessors, right here at the Texas DPS. Instead of relying on a flat rendering, she took pictures of the bare bones from the front and side, using the same standard tissue-depth markers that we apply when we build a bust. Then she enlarged the pictures to life size and filled in the flesh on paper, with an artist's eye. Pure computer renderings aren't nearly as good. They lack the spark of life that somebody like me can give them."

"I think I see what you mean." He'd wandered across the studio and was staring at some of the successful case studies she'd framed and hung on the walls. "These are amazing. The one in the middle is the 2-D picture?"

"Yes. That arrangement shows the original skull, then the drawing, then a photo of the final clay model."

"Plus the real person after an identification, right?"

"In the cases where I've been successful."

"What you do is really amazing." He watched her reaction as he asked, "How did you get started?"

"Not the way most people who know my history think," Paige said. "I was making posters and road signs for DPS when a Ranger happened to ask my boss if she knew anybody who could work with eyewitnesses to sketch from their descriptions. She recommended me—" Paige spread her arms to indicate the entire studio "—and here I am."

"That's the kind of drawing you did after the prowler grabbed you."

She pulled a face. "Yes. Not that it helped. I never did get a likeness that suited me."

"No, but we did eventually pull up a couple of blood samples from the grass."

"That DNA won't do much good without something to match it to. I've already heard it's not in the FBI's Combined DNA Index System." She glanced at the clay bust. "This man probably isn't in CODIS, either. Unless you can figure out who he was, there's little or no chance of coming up with a sample to test against for a match."

"Yeah. Hopefully, we'll know more as soon as you're done. Then I'll get out of your hair and you won't have to keep telling me to stop pacing."

He gave her a smile that he hoped was encouraging, though in his own heart he was anything but upbeat. It was hard for him to imagine not being around Paige. Not sharing a cup of hot coffee with her each morning. Not bidding her good-night every evening and knowing she was safe and sound in the motel room right next to his.

That was going to be one of the hardest adjustments. He'd want to know she was okay every second of every day and he'd have no way of being certain.

Oh, he supposed he could phone her, but even one daily call would probably be too much. It would certainly show her that his interest was a lot more than professional. And then what? What if she didn't want him keeping such close tabs on her and told him to buzz off?

Paige looked up from her work and smiled. "Why don't you go walk Max. That will give you something to do besides fidget."

"I never fidget."

"Hah! You're wound tighter than a two-dollar watch, as my grandpa used to say." Paige's expression grew tender, dreamy. "Grandpa was a darling. Even after…"

"Tell me more," Cade urged gently when she didn't go on. "It may help you to talk about it."

She rolled her eyes. "You mean tell you how my parents started screaming at each other all the time when there was no word on Amy? How my dad eventually got fed up and deserted us? How my mother muttered to herself constantly but stopped talking to other people, especially me?"

Coming closer, Cade perched a hip on her desk and nodded. "Yes. Like that, only different. What did you appreciate most about your grandfather?"

"That's easy. It was the way he treated me. He used to come over to the house and take me out for long walks, just the two of us. Sometimes we didn't talk at all and sometimes I told him about my schoolwork or a pet I dreamed of getting someday."

"Like Max?"

"Yes." She smiled over at the dog curled up next to a file cabinet, snoring. "I could never have imagined such a wonderful companion."

"You never had any pets as a child?"

Paige sobered. "No, never. Like I said before, my parents didn't think I was responsible enough."

"Your grandfather never said that, did he?"

"No." Her brow knit and she looked puzzled. "How did you know?"

"Just a good guess. When you finally make up your mind to talk to the Lord about it, remember your grandpa's great attitude, then magnify that a million times and you'll have a glimmer of the way God loves and accepts you."

He could tell by the way she pressed her lips into a thin line and lifted her chin that she wasn't yet ready to go that far. That was okay. He could wait, at least for a while. If he didn't happen to be nearby when Paige did finally decide to trust the Lord, he knew God would send someone else to give her a hug in his place.

The thought of Paige ending up in anyone else's arms sat in his stomach like last week's cold pizza. It didn't matter that he'd done this to himself by falling hopelessly in love, it still hurt like crazy. He didn't want to even consider Paige being comforted by anyone but him. Ever.

Figuring that the best course of action was to leave her office before he blurted out something he'd regret, he squared his hat on his head and touched the front of the brow. "I'll go walk your dog, *Miss Paige*. Lock this door behind us and stay put till we get back."

Half grimacing, half smiling, she raised her right hand and gave him a mock salute. "Yes, sir, Mr. Ranger, sir. Your wish is my command."

Cade figured the best way to respond was to mirror her actions so he waggled his eyebrows and grinned. "And don't you dare forget it."

By the time Cade returned, Paige had set aside her paper rendering and was rechecking the clay bust with calipers.

Captain Parker knocked, then stuck his head through her doorway to ask, "How's it going?"

"Fine," Paige said, continuing to concentrate on her work while she spoke. "Come on in. I'll show you."

Cade stepped aside, hovering close by.

"I'm giving the victim brown eyes," she told the captain, making a face at the model as if it were mocking her. "This part always creeps me out. It's like the victim is staring at me with those big, round, bugged-out, glass eyeballs. I like it much better once I've added lids and made the eyes look more natural."

"How soon will that be?" Parker asked.

"Muscles come first. I have to have the underneath structure right before I can add the skin and other details. Since the skull is Caucasoid and the approximate age is determined, too, it shouldn't take too long." She gestured toward her drafting table by tilting her head. "I did start a 2-D image over there. It's not quite finished, either. I'll have both for you soon."

The captain was twisting one side of his mustache, clearly deep in thought, as he studied her drawings. "Afraid he doesn't look familiar. At least not yet. We've sorted out the reports of missing persons from this area. I suppose he could also be a recruit that the Lions made through their subversive campaign to open the Mexican border." One eyebrow arched and he shot her a warning look. "Forget I said that, okay?"

"Okay." Paige stifled a giggle.

"Trouble is," Parker continued, "there's no way of telling if this fella was even a Texan. There wasn't anything identifiable buried with him. Just some clothing fragments."

"I know," Paige said. "The lab also said they found some short, brown hairs so I'll add that type of wig as a last detail."

"How much longer?" Parker asked.

Cade had been merely an observer until the captain stared pointedly at him. Then, he felt like he was being studied under a magnifying glass.

"Maybe two days. Maybe less." Paige's gaze followed that of her boss and also settled on the younger Ranger.

Parker was nodding. "Good. Well, don't let me keep you. There hasn't been any sign of activity around your house since you left so I've given your roommate permission to return anytime she's ready."

Paige's eyes widened and her head whipped around. She gaped, then snapped her jaw shut. "You told Angela to go back there? All by herself?"

"There's no good reason not to," the captain said flatly. "Ask Jarvis. He's been receiving daily reports from men in the field, Rangers and the sheriff's office alike. All their observations have been negative." He grinned. "You should be able to go home, too, if you want."

"Not yet," Cade interjected. He knew he shouldn't argue with his superior but where Paige was concerned he'd lost his usually level-headed perspective.

Captain Parker nodded knowingly and half smiled. "Calm down, Jarvis. I'm not going to terminate your assignment till Miss Paige is finished with her work. I've already let this nonsense go on longer than it should have, but I know how involved you are with Greg Pike's murder so I've let you hang around. When she's done, however, Captain Fritz wants you back in San Antonio ASAP, where you belong."

"Yes, sir." Cade's heart fell. He chanced a quick glance at Paige and immediately saw how worried she was.

"I need to get in touch with Angela. Stop her from going home," Paige said as soon as she and Cade were alone again. "I don't think for one minute it's as safe as the captain says."

"I agree."

She dug her cell out of her purse and used the speed dial to call her roommate, speaking to the voice mail recorder when it took the call. "Angela, it's me, Paige. Listen, I know they told you it was safe to go home but I don't think you should. Not yet. I'll be done with the job that seems to be causing all the trouble soon and then we'll talk. I'm at work. Call me?"

"You didn't get her?" Cade asked.

"No. I left a message." Chewing on her lower lip, Paige folded her arms across her chest and stared out the window, barely noticing the blustery November weather. "I'll feel better once I've spoken to her. She's a reasonable person. She'll understand."

"I hope so," Cade replied. "I've seen what these low-lifes are capable of." He gestured at the half-finished model. "Case in point."

Sighing, Paige considered the sculpture in progress. "I know what you mean. There's never been a victim who hasn't eventually talked to me." She cast him a slight smile. "I don't mean literally, of course."

Pausing, thoughtful, she gave the circular platform a little push and the clay model rotated as if the man she was reconstructing were turning his head.

Cade agreed. "He doesn't look very real yet but I do see what you mean. I sometimes get the same funny feeling when I'm working a crime scene."

When he paused and noisily cleared his throat, Paige began to scowl. "You look uncomfortable all of a sudden. Is there something you haven't told me?"

"Not about this case," Cade said.

"Then what?" Her eyes narrowed as she interpreted his unease. "Is it about Amy? Have you found new clues?"

As soon as she saw his crestfallen expression she realized that he'd tried and failed, just as she'd feared he would.

"I did look into it," the Ranger said. "I hoped…"

Paige interrupted. "So did I, for a long time. The trouble is, every time I hit another dead end I felt much worse. That's why I said I didn't want you to get involved. It's almost better not knowing than it is to be positive Amy's gone forever. Does that make sense to you?"

"Not really. I'll take your word for it."

"I still visualize her as she once was," Paige said, closing her eyes. "She's beautiful. Full of life. A blonde pixie with a twinkle in her blue eyes that warms my heart." She pointed to the ethereal-looking painting he'd remarked on the first time he'd visited her office. "*That's* how I choose to remember my little sister. Happy. Pretty. Enjoying life. When I play games with my memory it makes my loss more bearable."

"How about your folks?" Cade asked. "Even if they're estranged, wouldn't they prefer to know what ultimately became of her, if possible?"

"I don't know. Maybe. I haven't spoken to either of them for years." She raised a hand, palm out, to stop him from commenting. "It wasn't my doing, okay? They'd disowned me in their hearts long before Dad actually blurted it out to my face, but I knew. It was obvious."

"I'm so sorry."

"Thanks." She returned her attention to the sculpture

and eased it back to fully face her. "Now, suppose you boot up your laptop and find some other cases to occupy your time? I really do need to concentrate without interruption when I'm doing this kind of work."

"Of course. And Paige…?"

"Yes?"

The expression on his face confused her. Was it tenderness? Concern? Empathy? Her breath caught. Was it *pity?* Most likely. She felt the muscles in her neck and shoulders cramp.

Chin raised, eyes narrowing, she stared over at him and decided to speak her mind before he started expressing a sentiment that would make her very angry. "Look, Ranger, you and I both know I have very important work to complete. If you keep distracting me by dredging up my past, it's terribly counterproductive."

Swiveling her stool, she centered it in front of the bug-eyed model and dampened her fingertips before beginning to add thin, narrow strips of clay.

When she noted a slightly unsettling feeling and looked around again, she saw that Cade had quietly left the room.

To her dismay and surprise, she'd felt the lack of his presence keenly. It was as if someone had suddenly turned off the warmth of the sun.

FIFTEEN

It bothered Cade to realize that his concern wasn't wanted—or needed. Nevertheless, since Paige had spoken so plainly there was no doubt. She was clearly not open to the kind of emotional healing he was trying to explain, nor was she willing to turn to God and let Him work within her to bring eventual solace. That was too bad.

He stepped outside and was immediately chilled by the strong winter wind. Turning up the collar of his jacket he zipped it and squashed his hat on tighter so it wouldn't blow away. The sky was gray, the humidity high for Texas, even at this time of the year. It was a little too early for snow, not that they got that much this far south, anyway. Still, he'd better phone his dad and ask him to double-check the ranch, just in case.

Standing in the shelter of a recessed doorway, Cade used his cell. He was about to leave a message when the call was finally answered with a breathless, "Hello?"

"Hey, Dad, it's me. I was just wondering how the weather is down there."

"Nasty," Jacob said. "I was out closing up the barn when I heard the phone ringing."

"I'm glad you're back. I remembered you were off on one of your volunteer building trips for the church and I wondered when you were coming home. How did it go?"

"Fine. We got a lot accomplished for those poor folks. Don't worry. One of my friends came out here every day to feed and water the stock in case you had to be away, too."

"Thanks. I thought I might drop by when we were down that way a week or so ago but it didn't work out."

"We?" The older man snorted. "This story is gettin' interesting. Who was with you?"

"Paige Bryant," Cade said, pausing for the reaction he suspected would follow.

"From the cold case you asked me about?"

"Yeah. We came down to use the lab equipment instead of waiting for hers to be replaced or repaired. Somebody trashed her studio."

"How's the girl doing after that?"

"She's not a girl anymore, Dad, remember? She's a grown woman. And a pretty one, too. I just…"

"Spit it out. Let's have the real reason you're calling me."

"Is it that obvious?"

"It is to me. You and I think alike. You gettin' sweet on her?"

"You could say that, I guess."

"Never mind what I say. What do *you* say?"

Cade cupped his free hand around the instrument before he confessed, "I can't imagine my life without her in it."

"Uh-oh. What does she have to say about that?"

"I haven't told her yet. It's complicated."

"Have you prayed about it?"

"In a manner of speaking. There have been a few times lately when all I've had time to do is act. That's part of the problem. I'm afraid she's seeing me as some kind of superhero instead of as a regular guy."

"You *are* a Texas Ranger. That's pretty special."

"Yeah, well, I think it's a lot more than that. I've literally had to rescue her more than once and she's reacted as if what I did was out of the ordinary." He cleared his throat. "Funny thing is, it seemed pretty special to me, too, at the time."

"That's because it was. The Lord works in mysterious ways, you know."

Cade could tell from his father's tone that the older man was grinning and he felt his cheeks warming in spite of the chilly wind. "Paige and I haven't really known each other that long. I just know I'm going to miss her a lot when I have to leave Austin. We've been spending almost every waking moment together since she started working on the latest facial reconstruction."

"Sounds to me like you two probably know each other better than some couples who've dated for months, if you count by the total hours instead of thinking of it as dating."

That was the first time Cade had considered that aspect of his time with Paige. They were probably more well acquainted already than he had been with other women he might have considered proposing to.

Proposing? He gasped, choked and started to cough.

On the other end of the line, Jacob was gleefully chortling. "Simmer down, son. I fell for your mama in the blink of an eye but it took her a tad longer to see what a wonderful husband I'd make. She was worth waitin' for."

"Meaning, don't rush things?"

"Hey, don't ask me. I'm no psychologist. And I can't say I've ever been able to figure out women, except maybe your mama. We sure did have some good times together, Maryanne and me."

"I know you did. I'd like to have that kind of marriage someday. I guess that's why I called, although if you'd asked me before we started talking, I wouldn't have realized it."

"Just trust the good Lord," Jacob said. "He'll work it out for you."

"Yeah, I suppose so." Cade shivered and hunched his shoulders with his back to the worst of the wind. "You'd better stay in the house till this storm passes," he warned. "It's not looking good here."

"Here, either. Take care of yourself, son. We still on for Thanksgiving dinner?"

"Sure. I should be home for keeps by then. Pick up a turkey and we'll deep fry it—outside on the porch. The other fixings we can get at the deli."

"Good plan. No sense takin' a chance of setting the house on fire with the turkey cooker the way some folks do. Why don't you ask Paige to join us? The more the merrier."

"Maybe." *And maybe not.* "Bye, Dad."

Smiling as he pictured his macho father with kitchen mitts on both hands, carefully lowering a turkey into a boiling kettle of peanut oil, Cade sighed. They'd have a good time, as always, but no holiday had seemed as festive, as complete, since his early teenage years when his mother had still been alive.

Cade rejected Jacob's suggestion several times before finally giving in. *Okay.* He'd ask Paige to share their holiday meal. Since she didn't have close family to celebrate with, it was actually possible she'd accept. It was worth a try.

Turning, Cade slid the temporary key card he'd been issued through the scanner and unlocked the entrance door. Now that he'd decided, it was all he could do to keep from hurrying back to Paige and inviting her immediately.

That notion was so patently stupid it almost made him laugh. If he'd learned anything about her in the past days and weeks, it was that she was not the type to act without thinking things through very carefully. The more chances he gave her to come up with a good excuse to avoid coming for dinner, the less likely it would be that she'd agree. That meant he'd have to bide his time and keep his mouth shut until almost Thanksgiving day.

Cade grinned and rubbed his palms together to warm his hands. Paige would join them. He'd see to it somehow. And when she did, she'd experience belonging to a loving family. It was a personal connection that she needed, that she was lacking. If he could coax her out of her shell, even for one family affair, perhaps she'd see how well she fit into his life—into his future.

Paige had tried repeatedly to reach Angela and had grown so frustrated she was ready to scream. She was ending another voice mail message when Cade returned.

"What's up?" he nodded at the cell phone in her hand.

"I can't get hold of Angie. I'm worried."

"Maybe she's out on another flight."

"That was my first thought. I checked with her airline. They wouldn't tell me anything." She eyed the nearly completed bust. "What time is it?"

"After seven. You ready to call it a day? We could grab another pizza."

Paige was heading for the sink against the back wall to wash her hands. "Let me get this clay off first, then we'll go."

"To supper?"

"No." She gave him a look that plainly said she wasn't in the mood to agree with anything he said. "We're going to check the house to make sure my friend isn't in danger."

"Nope."

Bristling, Paige stared at him. "Oh, yeah? Watch me."

"You can't. You don't have wheels."

"Thanks to you. Captain Parker phoned and told me my truck has been ready for ages. Did you just happen to forget to mention that?" Whipping off her soiled plastic apron she hung it on a peg by the sink. "If you won't drive me, I'll walk over to the garage and pick up my truck. Either way, I'm going to go look for Angela."

"The weather's bad out there and getting worse by the minute. Why don't we just have the sheriff cruise by and see if she went home?"

"Then what? Are they going to stay with her 24/7? Suppose they warn her to leave and she chooses to listen to Captain Parker's advice, instead? I would, wouldn't you?"

"Yes."

"Then what's your problem, Ranger?"

Raking his fingers through his short, blond hair he shook his head. "You are, lady. How do you expect me to keep you safe if you insist on taking chances by leaving the areas we know are secure?"

That was all the opening she needed to make her point so she said, "I thought you were trusting the Lord?"

"I am. That doesn't mean I intend to stuff a swarm of killer bees into my shirt just to see what God will do about it."

She grabbed her jacket and started to sidle past him as she threaded her arms into the sleeves.

Cade reached for her. Stopped her. His touch on her shoulders was firm but nevertheless gentle.

"We'll go." He cast a quick glance at the nearly complete sculpture. "Just keep in mind that you have an important job to finish."

"I never forget my job."

"I know. Sometimes I almost wish you would."

Paige was flabbergasted. One minute they'd been arguing and then suddenly his mood had changed completely. Judging by the way he was now gazing into her eyes and cupping her shoulders, she suspected he was about to bend over and kiss her! Would she mind? Not in the least. As a matter of fact...

Warmth infused her cheeks and Paige knew she was blushing. Truth to tell, it looked as if Cade was, too.

Her lips parted slightly. She started to raise on tiptoe and tilt her head to one side.

Then, he suddenly set her away from him and let go. Paige was so surprised by the abruptness of his moves she staggered. Blinking rapidly, she watched him square his hat on his head and fist his keys as if he intended to leave without her.

"Hey! Wait for me," Paige said, her voice raised. "I need to put some of this stuff back in the safe before I go anywhere."

"Well, hurry it up. The sooner we check your house, the sooner I can get you locked up in the motel."

The old grouch was back. Lovely. Not that she was feeling any more amiable than he was. One thing was certain, she concluded. She had not been the only one thinking of kissing and being kissed. The real question was, why had Cade backed away instead of acting on the obvious mutual attraction?

Because he doesn't really want to be involved with me, she answered, sobering. It was one thing to find someone appealing and quite another for an honorable man like Cade Jarvis to take the chance of leading her on when he'd decided they could never have a romantic relationship. He was the consummate gentleman. A true Texas Ranger.

Paige just wished he wasn't quite so conscientious when it came to a simple display of affection.

Her thoughts centered on the way she felt about Cade. She had been the one to cling to him after the highway fiasco, to hug his waist in the restaurant parking lot and later hold his hand. It was all her idea. She couldn't recall one specific thing the Ranger had done to demonstrate that he shared her loving feelings.

Chagrined and more than a little embarrassed to recall the way she'd behaved, she grabbed Max's leash, locked the safe and her office door and hurried after Cade. Should she apologize? she wondered. Maybe try to explain or laugh it all off?

That answer was easy. If she even hinted that she'd expected a kiss and then found out he had purposely avoided giving her one, she would be humiliated. Worse, their working relationship would be weakened, if not totally destroyed.

How about later? she asked herself. *Perhaps. No, probably.* Cade had squeezed her fingers as they left the restaurant, and even before that he'd voluntarily eased the cramped muscles in her neck. He must be at least slightly attracted to her. That was good, right?

Leaning into the wind and dragging her reluctant, shivering dog along, Paige gritted her teeth. Max wasn't the only one who disliked thunderstorms. When lightning was involved, it often knocked out power to whole blocks of the city and brought the total darkness she hated so.

"At least it hasn't started to rain yet," she remarked, sliding out of the way and shoving the dog onto the floor at her feet. "Wet sheepdog is not a pleasant smell."

Cade didn't comment. He hadn't said a single word to her since they'd left the office and it didn't look as if he planned to get talkative anytime soon.

Fine. If he wanted to sulk, let him. As long as he kept his promise to take her to the house to check on Angie, she didn't care if he clammed up like a—like a clam.

A handsome clam in a white cowboy hat, she added, chagrined.

There was no getting around it. She was a goner. She'd fallen for the guy so hard she was hardly able to think straight, let alone make sense of her life outside the studio.

What was it Cade had said, exactly? That he wanted her to forget about her job? That couldn't have been what he'd meant. They were both dedicated to the Texas Rangers to the point of obsession. There was no way Cade Jarvis had told her to forget it.

Another thing she wasn't about to forget was this special time with him, Paige added, lowering her lashes and sneaking a sideways peek at his profile while he drove. When he was sent back to San Antonio, she knew she was going to mourn the loss of his companionship nearly as deeply as she'd once mourned for her sister.

Averting her face, Paige stared out the window, not focusing on the view. Instead, she was picturing the two people whom she loved with all her heart and imagining how painful it would be to bid goodbye to the only one who remained. In Amy's case she'd had no choice. Did she with Cade?

A tear slipped over her lower lashes and trickled down her cheek. Whatever she eventually said or did, she was going to make certain he didn't feel trapped or coerced simply because they'd become friends while working together. Until she'd heard him express equal affection, in so many words, she was not going to let him suspect she loved him.

That ridiculous assumption almost made her smile. Not let him know? How could he help seeing it? She'd practically thrown herself at the poor man back in her office.

Yes, and he should have given in and kissed me, Paige told herself firmly. Hey! Maybe he was a lousy kisser and finding that out would have ended her infatuation.

Talk about ridiculous. If there was one thing she was sure of, it was that Cade Jarvis was the best kisser in all of Texas. The proof was in heart.

SIXTEEN

Cade heard Paige's phone start to jingle a few minutes before they reached her house. He listened while she answered excitedly. "Hello?" Frowning, she looked over at him. "I can't hear anybody."

"Do you have caller ID?"

"Yes, but the number is listed as private."

"Terrific."

"Hey, don't blame me." Clapping her free hand over her other ear she repeated, "Hello? Hello?"

"Still can't hear anything?"

"No."

"Then hang up. We're here."

He doused his headlights, killed the engine and coasted silently into the driveway. Theirs wasn't the only vehicle present.

"That's Angela's car!"

"Okay. You stay here while I go have a look."

"No way. She has to be home."

"Does she? There are no lights showing inside the house. Maybe she's on a date." He gestured at the small phone still in Paige's hand. "I need you to sit right here in case whoever called before does it again. For all we know, your friend might have been trying to check in with you and just had a weak signal."

"Do you actually believe that?"

"It's as plausible as any ideas you've come up with." He leaned low to peer through the windshield at the stormy sky. "Lightning might have interfered with the connection, too."

"Yeah, right."

"Do you know how to shoot?" Cade asked, purposely changing the subject and giving her a stern look for added effect.

"Only with a camera. Why?"

"Because I was thinking of leaving a gun with you for protection. Since you aren't proficient with firearms there's no way I'd do that." He held out his hand. "Give me your house keys."

When she hesitated, he added, "Be sensible for once, Paige. You can't take Max out in this weather. Look at him. He's shaking so hard the whole truck is vibrating."

"Aren't you worried about leaving *me?*"

"I won't be far away. And you have the horn as well as your cell phone. If you feel threatened, just honk loud to let me know you're scared, then dial 911 and request backup. Remember to lock the door."

As soon as she'd finished grumbling unintelligibly and had given in, Cade swapped his trademark white hat for her keys, then slid silently out of the truck. He closed the door with care instead of slamming it. Rangers weren't often involved in this kind of regular police action but he was well versed in all procedures.

His one and only concern was for the woman he was

leaving behind in his truck. If they started spending time together off the job, as he hoped they would, he was going to teach Paige self-defense, including how to shoot to protect herself without blowing a hole in her own foot.

Approaching the house slowly, he peered in the front window, then signaled to Paige to indicate where he intended to go next. He couldn't see anything inside his truck except shadows, which was just as well since he didn't want anyone else to know she was even there.

Gun drawn and ready, Cade flipped on his flashlight then started around the corner of the small home and entered the backyard, just as he had when searching for clues to the previous prowler.

The short hair on the back of his neck prickled and he froze to listen. It was too late in the year for the chirps of crickets or locusts. Birds were essentially silent, too. In the distance, a dog howled. Another answered. Other than that, all he could hear was the whistling wind and the repeated rumble of distant thunder. Lightning lit the clouds as if there were a spotlight flashing behind them. At times, the entire sky seemed to pulse and glow.

Thankful he was no longer wearing a hat that would have made him as visible as a jet black horse in a field of snow, he tiptoed up to the back porch and tried the knob.

Locked. He located the proper key on the first try, inserted and turned it.

In seconds, he was inside.

Paige hadn't felt unusually nervous until she'd lost sight of Cade. When her phone jingled again the noise made her jump. Before she could speak, however, she heard a voice whisper, "It's me, Don't hang up again."

"Angie? I can hardly hear you."

"I can't talk louder."

"Why not?"

"Because he'll hear me."

Paige clasped the little phone so tightly her hand ached. "Who will? Where are you?"

"At the house. I came…"

"Angie?" Paige's voice raised. "Angela. Answer me!"

"Shush. Not so loud. I can hear him walking down the hallway."

"Listen, Angie," Paige said, fighting to remain calm for her friend's sake. "There's a Ranger in there right now. Maybe that's who you hear."

"There is?"

"Yes. He's tall and kind of blond. I gave him my keys so he could let himself in and check on you. He has a flashlight."

"Hang on while I look."

Paige held the line *and* her breath. There were indistinguishable, muted sounds in the background. Shuffling. A slight thud, as if a door were closing.

Time stood still. Thunder rumbled. "Angie? Talk to me. What just happened? Hello? Hello?"

Shivering, she peered through the pickup's windows. Enormous drops of rain were beginning to fall. There was no illumination in the yard except that from the streetlights down the block and the irregularly spaced lightning strikes. It wasn't pitch black out there but it sure wasn't as bright as she liked it to be when she had to venture into the yard at night.

Cade had disappeared around the house. That meant he'd probably already used her keys to enter through the kitchen and his were the footsteps Angie had heard.

So, where were they now? Why hadn't they come right out and told her everything was fine? And why couldn't she spot an occasional glow from his flashlight through the windows?

"Good question," she muttered, disgusted and short of patience. That bossy, stubborn Ranger knew how worried she'd be, yet he'd left her behind to cool her heels while he took his sweet time checking the house and yard.

Just then, Max alerted. A low growl shook his whole body and he stiffened, pressing his nose to the crack between the door and the chassis.

"Easy, boy. He'll be back soon."

Max didn't act as if he believed a word she'd said. Neither did Paige. The house was compact enough that Cade should have been able to *crawl* through every room by now, let alone walk. And if Angela had shown herself, they should both have realized it was safe to come out.

She scooted behind the steering wheel. Her hand rested on the door handle. Her fingers tightened around it. *Go? Stay?*

Paige stared at her phone. It still showed a connection. She held it to her ear and shouted, "Angela! What's going on? Talk to me!"

A wild-eyed, dark-haired young woman burst out of the closet. In one fluid movement, Cade centered her in the flashlight's narrow beam and leveled his gun.

She held up her hands and screamed. "Don't shoot!"

"Are you Angela?"

"Yes," she said, sobbing and grasping the arm holding the light. "Turn that off so nobody can see us. We have to get out of here. Now."

"Why?" Every sense primed, Cade sandwiched the trembling young woman between himself and the closet she'd just vacated while he trained his .45 on the darkness beyond. "What's going on?"

"I don't know. All the lights went out. I heard somebody sneaking around so I hid."

"Where did the sounds come from?"

"The kitchen, I think."

"I just came through there. I didn't run into anybody. How about the front of the house? Did you hear anything in that direction?"

"No. Only you coming down the hall. I phoned Paige and she told me you were in here."

"That was *you* on her cell?"

"Yes. She hung up the first time."

"That was my fault," Cade said quietly. "Are you steady enough to walk with me?"

"I—I think so. Just get me out of here."

"Start for the front door." He slipped one arm around her waist so he could control her movements and steer her out of the path of his gun in case he had to fire. "I'll be right beside you. Let's go."

It was Max's mounting frenzy that tipped the balance for Paige. She trusted that dog's instincts far more than she trusted her own—or those of any other human being, except maybe the Ranger who had ordered her to stay precisely where he'd left her.

What if something bad had happened to him? Or what if he and Angie were both in trouble? There hadn't been another peep out of her phone. Not since she'd told her friend to look for Cade.

Rain was now hitting the windshield so fiercely it was forming a solid sheet of water and making it even harder for Paige to see what was going on outside the truck.

Her fingers tightened. The door handle moved slightly. Max apparently assumed she was about to let him out because he crouched and gathered himself like a steeple-chase horse preparing to run an obstacle course.

"No," Paige said firmly. "Sit. Stay."

He did nothing of the kind. Not only did he redouble his efforts to get out by scratching at the floor, he began to bark so loudly it hurt Paige's ears.

"I said, *no!*" Grabbing his collar, she forced him back so she could swing her legs between him and the door and block his escape as she pulled the handle.

The locking mechanism had barely released when Max lunged past her and threw his full weight against the door panel.

Paige lost her hold.

Rocketing out, the dog hit the ground running, then made such a quick, tight turn, his claws tore up the soggy grass and threw puddled water higher than his own back.

"No!"

She made one futile grab for him and missed. Thunder rolled. Her frantic calls were muted by the roar of the rapidly worsening storm. In seconds, her hair was plastered to her head and there was so much water running down her face she could barely see.

Temporarily stunned, she just stood there muttering, "What have I done?"

The next zigzag of electricity hit the ground so close to Paige she felt a prickling of the fine hairs on her arms and the nape of her neck. There wasn't enough elapsed time between the crackling of the lightning and its ensuing boom for her to count to *one,* let alone further.

She'd instinctively ducked and covered herself as best she could with her arms. Now, she straightened and pushed her wet hair out of her eyes. If she had to choose between running for cover or standing there like a dummy and playing the part of a human lightning rod, it was not hard to decide which action was best.

Lifting her denim jacket just enough to pull the back of the collar over her head for what little protection it offered, she faced into the slanted, wind-driven downpour and started around the house.

Cade and Angela had made it down the hallway and almost to the living room when he felt her tense. He knew why. He'd heard a faint sound in the background, too. It wasn't easy to pinpoint or evaluate. Nevertheless, something had caught their attention.

He wasn't going to hang around and try to figure out what. That could wait until he'd delivered Angela to Paige and had made sure his backup was on the way.

"Open the door slowly," Cade murmured, once again shoving her ahead to make himself her literal bodyguard. The sound of the lock releasing as she turned the knob was one of the most welcome things he'd heard in a long time.

Angela did as she was told. Cade restrained her to keep her from bolting though the doorway before he'd had a chance to check the immediate area.

The flashlight swept over the narrow, covered porch and down the walkway. "Okay. All clear."

Once outside, he continued to control her movements. "See that white truck in the driveway? That's where we're going. Paige is waiting for you."

The young woman let out a whimper and sagged against him, making it necessary for Cade to either holster his .45 for safety's sake or let her drop into a heap at his feet. Since they were in the clear, at least for the present, he decided to swing her into his arms and carry her.

"I'm glad you didn't faint while we were still inside," Cade mumbled, staring at the sheeting rain between them and the dry cab of the truck.

He figured it was better to see that Angela was quickly and safely delivered to Paige than to take the chance that the headstrong artist would decide to come fetch her roommate. Besides, he was worried about the strong possibility of damaging hail being mixed in with the rain. Getting wet was bad enough. Being hit in the head by gobs of ice the size of golf balls was far worse. That kind of foul weather had been known to knock a full-grown steer senseless.

In less than fifteen long strides he reached the driver's door of the truck. Assuming that Paige could now see him, even in the near dark, he paused. The door didn't open. He kicked it with his boot.

"Hey! Open up. We're drowning out here and I can't reach my keys."

Nothing happened. Then lightning flashed. In that split second of illumination, Cade saw enough to realize that his worst fears had come true. The cab of the truck was empty.

Paige discovered the kitchen door ajar and blamed Cade, scowling when she noted a glistening trail of water on the tile.

She kept staring at that same part of the floor, waiting for another flash to allow her to see where to safely step. Although that flooring was pretty, it could be as slippery as ice when it was wet. And right now, parts of it were sopping.

Out of patience in seconds, Paige extended her arms and groped her way to the counter. There was a penlight in the drawer where she and Angela tossed all the odd items they had no better place for. Once she laid hands on that, assuming its batteries weren't dead, she'd feel much better

"Almost there," Paige whispered. She was trembling as much from being soaked to the skin as she was from fright—or so she kept telling herself. She figured, as long as she concentrated on what she was trying to accomplish and didn't allow herself to dwell on the fact that her surroundings were so dark, she'd be okay.

She had to be. The most important people in her life might need her help.

Why wasn't she there yet? She took one more small, sideways step. Her hip bumped into something hard. Puzzled, she reached down. It was the drawer she'd been seeking. It was also *open*. Paige held her breath. That wasn't normal. Neither she nor Angela could stand leaving cupboards or things like that ajar, so why was this drawer not neatly closed?

Something crashed and startled her. It sounded as if glass had broken in another part of the house. "Max? Is that you, boy?" she called softly, tentatively.

Waiting and straining to listen, she heard the familiar padding of her pet's paws, first coming down the hall, then on the tile as his nails clacked against the harder surface.

A flash from the sky outside highlighted his white markings. It *was* him! Paige held out a hand. "Max! Oh, Max, am I glad to see you. Where have you been?" She knelt to hug him in spite of his dripping coat while he licked her cheek.

Moments later, her knees might have buckled if she had not already been at floor level.

A sinister-sounding, male voice spoke from the direction of the archway leading into the hall. "Do not worry. I have been taking good care of him, Señorita." Then, the man laughed as if he'd just told a dirty joke.

Paige gasped and gritted her teeth to keep from screaming. Every nerve tightened. Every sense was on overload. She grabbed a handful of Max's ruff to hold him back as he shifted to face the speaker and began to growl.

I know that laugh, she realized without having to mull it over. This was the same man who had grabbed her when she'd been in the yard looking for Max. What else was he responsible for? And why had he singled her out?

It took another few seconds for his use of Spanish

to register in her racing thoughts. The Lions of Texas were said to be recruiting Mexican nationals to do their dirty work by promising to legally open the border. From what she could remember of this man's face, he could be Hispanic, although her sketch had ended up looking more like the one she'd done for Corinna Pike several months ago. The lowlife who had stalked Corinna was in jail. Therefore, this had to be somebody else.

Standing slowly, Paige gathered her courage and waited. If she could get one more good look at this man's face, her chances of successfully drawing him would definitely increase.

Yeah, if I live that long, she countered silently. Should she talk to him? Keep quiet? *What?*

To her right, in the direction of the outside door, she thought she heard a floorboard squeak. Was he over there now? Had he moved so stealthily he'd already cut off her closest means of escape?

There was only one way to tell. "Why are you doing this to me?" she demanded, surprised at the strength and steadiness of her voice.

"It is my job. And you have caused me much trouble."

That answer came from the place where she'd last heard him. Did that mean there was someone else making noise over by the door? And if there was, how could she find out if it was Cade? It could just as easily be a henchman of the guy who was threatening her.

If so, her chances of survival had just hit rock bottom.

SEVENTEEN

When Cade had discovered his truck empty he'd tried the door and found it unlocked. Placing the semiconscious Angela on the seat, he took care to tuck in her feet before he slammed and locked the door. There was no way he could possibly watch both women unless they were all together, and since this one was now out of imminent danger, he'd have to take the chance she'd stay that way.

He was finishing his call for backup as he circled the house for the second time. He didn't intend to wait until other officers arrived. Paige was probably inside. And where she was, Max likely was. It would be easier to spot the partly white dog than to locate her, especially if she happened to be hiding the way Angela had been.

"That's assuming Paige knows what she's walked into," he said under his breath. Chances were she didn't have a clue. Truth to tell, neither did he. He just hoped and prayed he'd be able to reach her before someone else beat him to it.

Rounding the back of the house, he was positive he heard Paige's voice. His momentary relief was quickly replaced by dread. That wasn't the dog she was talking to, and judging by the other person's accent, whoever it was had to be either Hispanic or a very good mimic.

Gun drawn, he started to climb the rear porch steps. The second board he touched squeaked under his weight like a rusty hinge. Cade froze with one booted foot raised. He hadn't noticed that noise in the past. Since everything out there was now soaked, perhaps that was why the slight shifting of the wood had given away his presence.

He waited, listening to his heartbeats pounding in his ears and praying that no one else had heard. All he could think to ask was, *Please, Lord, let me be in time.*

Nothing happened. Nothing moved, inside or out, except for tumbling, loose leaves and the copious amounts of water being carried along by the gale. Although he was soaked and freezing, Cade gave thanks that the storm's rumbling had covered his misstep.

Continuing to place each foot slowly, cautiously, he finally reached the doorway. Because he didn't know where Paige was or how bad the situation might be, he didn't dare risk turning on his flashlight or going any closer. Not yet.

What he yearned to do was burst into the kitchen and attack. To save Paige. To hold her in his arms again and never let go.

Instead, he took a deep breath and steeled himself for whatever was to come.

"I warn you. I'm armed," Paige shouted. This time, she was chagrined to hear far less confidence in her tone.

"I will take my chances, Señorita."

"I got away from you before. I can do it again." She

swallowed hard, wishing her throat didn't feel as if it was stuffed with dry cotton. "Did you bring help this time? You'll need it."

The man's low, ominous chuckle made her skin crawl. When he said, "I can handle a stupid woman like you with one *mano* tied behind my back," she had the answer she'd sought. He was alone.

Her thoughts refused to coalesce into anything she considered sensible. Whether Cade was close by or not, her problem was still how to reach the back door and escape before being attacked. With her heart already racing and her legs feeling as though somebody had made off with all her bones when she wasn't looking, running for her life was out of the question.

What if she crawled? Success would depend entirely upon a continuing lack of light to reveal her movements. The unpredictable flashes from the storm did seem to be lessening but there was still plenty of thunder rolling in the distance, making it impossible to predict the future. Still, what choice did she have? She couldn't just stand there like a brainless mannequin.

Holding fast to the counter for support, Paige bent her knees and eased herself toward the floor. Max had already swiveled to look toward the door.

The moment Paige released her hold, he made a beeline for the door and disappeared. She could only hope that he'd sensed Cade because his swift movement had caused her antagonist to curse loudly and hurl something in the dog's direction. Whatever it was landed with a hollow thwack and gave a slight bounce.

Paige was crawling, feeling her way with her hands. The tile was still dry wherever she touched, meaning she had not yet come close enough to the exit.

A louder, more colorful string of shouted expletives was suddenly interrupted by a hard-sounding thud and a distinctive Spanish phrase that she wouldn't have dreamed of translating, no matter what.

"Freeze! Texas Rangers," was shouted from the doorway.

Paige hunkered down next to the cabinets and waited, expecting the explosion of gunfire at any moment.

Instead, she heard sounds of slapping, cursing and scrambling. Drops of water showered her. The attacker had evidently stepped in the puddles Max had tracked in and her slick floor tile had claimed another victim.

She knew Cade had to be close and hoped it had not been he who had fallen. "Watch out for the water on the floor," she shouted. "It's real slippery. I think it knocked him down."

"Where?"

"Center of the room," Paige answered.

Cade's flashlight blinked on. He pointed it at the area she'd indicated. All that was visible was a lot of scattered water and a baseball bat that didn't belong there. The prowler himself was gone.

Cade knew that keeping Paige with him would hamper his ability to search. However, he decided he'd rather know exactly where she was than try to apprehend a criminal who already had a good head start. He'd leave that man to the patrol cars he could hear arriving, their sirens howling. Besides, Cade reasoned, if he left Paige alone, the culprit might double back and have another chance to harm her.

Taking charge, Cade grasped her upper arm. Together, they followed a trail of damp footprints that led through the house and out the front door.

"Where's Angie?" Paige asked in a tremulous voice. "Did he get her?"

"No. I did."

"But…"

"She's in the truck." Cade glowered. Right now, right here, he was so angry he was almost afraid to speak.

He didn't slacken his grip until they had reached the pickup and he'd seen that all his charges were safely locked inside. Then, he turned to greet the approaching police officers.

Cade blew a heavy sigh as he ran his fingers through his wet hair and pushed it back. He was soaked to the skin. He was tired of having to ask for help. He was fed up with trying to keep tabs on a headstrong woman who seemed bent on self-destruction. And he was disgusted with himself for letting said woman get under his skin. She did nothing but drive him crazy and cause him grief.

"So what's my problem?" he muttered under his breath. "A few more days and I'll be back home."

Without Paige Bryant, his conscience added. Although that fact had first seemed inconsequential, then later had begun to make him believe he might be in love, he now realized it was simply the way things had to be. He lived and worked in San Antonio. She had to stay in Austin. They were not only separated by their obviously incompatible personalities, they would soon have many miles of Texas roads between them, too.

"And then I'll be able to stop thinking about her all the time," Cade insisted.

He told himself he believed it, too. Well, sort of.

* * *

Paige was so exhausted from her ordeal she was sure she'd sleep well that night. Unfortunately, disturbing thoughts concerning Cade kept her awake till almost dawn. She'd never seen anyone as angry as he'd been when he'd found her cornered in the kitchen.

After the sheriff's deputies had checked her house to make sure no one was hiding inside, she and Cade had delivered Angie to an emergency room for a checkup. There, doctors had insisted on keeping the young woman for observation. Paige had refused to submit herself to the same scrutiny, even though Cade had acted as if he'd wanted her to agree to anything that would keep her out of his hair.

"One more hard day should do it," she'd told him after they'd seen Angela settled. "I'll definitely be done with the reconstruction by tomorrow evening, if not sooner. I'm not going to waste time lying in a hospital bed when there's work to be done."

That had apparently been a logical enough argument to convince him. He had driven her back to the motel and left her at her door without even saying good-night. She knew she'd upset him, but surely they could have talked it all out if they'd tried. Instead, he'd been acting like a spoiled brat throwing a tantrum.

Hoping he'd have cooled off by morning, she was flabbergasted when she started to leave her room the next day and found him right outside. He was seated on the ground, wrapped in a blanket, with his back propped against her door. His hat was tilted over his eyes.

Paige gave a little gasp of surprise. "Were you there all night?"

"Yup," he said, righting the hat. "I've learned my lesson. Can't trust you to stay put."

"Don't be ridiculous. You must be half-frozen. At least come in and let me make you a cup of hot coffee."

"No, thanks." He got to his feet and stretched as he eyed her fresh clothing. "You ready to go?"

"Almost. I was just going to knock on your door and ask you to walk Max while I brushed my hair."

The hard glance he gave her in response hurt all the way to her toes. She'd told him the absolute truth and he was looking at her as if she were the biggest, boldest liar he'd ever met.

"Okay," Paige said, taking a step with the dog at heel. "Suit yourself. The longer we hang around here wasting time, the longer it will be before I finish that face for you."

He shed the blanket and held out a hand. "Give him to me. Just make it quick." Taking a step away while Max tugged on the other end of the leash, he added, "And don't try anything. I'll be watching your door every second."

Paige was so taken aback she couldn't come up with a snappy retort. Why bother trying? As things stood, she figured the best thing to do was ignore him, although doing that went against her nature. It didn't seem right to accept his censure without trying to explain.

Explain what? Obviously, she'd made him livid by doing what she'd thought at the time was the right thing. There was no way to relive last night and change her actions. Besides, she hadn't done or said anything wrong. Not really. Why couldn't he see how pure her motives were, how tender her feelings were—how deeply his silence was hurting her?

If she hadn't been so utterly in love with the man she wouldn't have cared how put out he was. But because she did care, with all her heart, she knew she couldn't let him just drive away once her work was finished. There had to be some way to convince him to forgive her first. There had to be.

Those thoughts took her back to her childhood, to the way she'd often felt like an outsider. A useless member of a hopelessly fractured family. Back then, she'd simply accepted it as her lot in life.

Not this time, Paige vowed. She'd experienced a taste of what it meant to belong, to be accepted just as she was, and it was high time she reminded that stubborn Ranger of his own words about forgiveness.

Pausing, she closed her eyes and recalled her kindly grandfather exactly the way Cade had suggested. "If You're really like Gramps, God, You're going to have to show me because I don't understand any of this. You gave me a sister to love, then took her away. Are You going to take Cade, too, or is there something I can do to make things right between us? Tell me? Please?" A catch in her throat stopped her from going any further.

Sniffling, she opened her eyes and went to the bathroom sink to splash cold water on her face. She was not going to lose control. She was not going to cry.

Reflected in the vanity mirror, Paige saw more than the image of the capable, talented career woman she'd expected. She also saw a glimmer of hope. That was enough to make her smile and wonder. It seemed impossible that it could be that easy to connect with her heavenly Father when churches had insisted for thousands of years that they were the only way to reach Him.

Paige straightened and ran the brush through her hair one more time. She grinned at the mirror. "Okay, God," she said, "I'll give it another shot. I do want to believe the same way I used to when I was a kid. It just seemed so much easier to do back then. Being an adult is very confusing."

Turning off the lights, she picked up her purse and headed for the door. "Being in love with Cade Jarvis is even worse," she whispered to herself. "Figuring out the secrets of the universe has to be easier than understanding that Ranger. Especially since last night."

Cade's pulse jumped the instant Paige reappeared. He tugged on Max's collar and pointed. "There she is, old boy. Let's go."

More than eager, the sheepdog bounded toward her as fast as the taut leash would allow. Fortunately for Cade, the tether was long enough that he didn't have to do more than jog to keep up till the dog reached both the truck and its master.

Cade stood back while Paige greeted her pet as if they'd been parted for years and had desperately missed each other the whole time. He knew what that felt like, if only by imagining his future.

"We'll swing by the garage and pick up your truck today," he said flatly as he held the door for her. "I'm sure it'll feel good to have your own transportation."

"Yes. It will."

He figured he might as well go on, explain the necessary details and get it all over with. "I've booked your room here for the rest of the week," he said, "just in case you need it."

"I see. What about my house? What about Angela? We both have to live somewhere."

"We expect to get good prints from the bat the guy dropped in your kitchen. Once we know who he is, I'm sure we'll have him in custody in no time."

"What if you don't? What if his fingerprints aren't in IAFIS because he's never been caught before?"

"Don't borrow trouble," Cade said, giving her a scowl. To his surprise, Paige chuckled low instead of staying serious.

"Borrow it?" she said with arched brows. "I don't have to borrow a thing. I have plenty of trouble that's my very own."

He set his jaw. She was right, of course. She had enough problems for a dozen people. Once she finished her current assignment and they were able to ID the victim, however, he was pretty sure she'd be in the clear. That was even more likely since her attacker had told her he was merely doing a job.

What if that job included murder instead of just slowing her work? Cade asked himself. He'd spent a lot of time last night, while he was leaned against her door, praying that this case would wrap up satisfactorily before he had to leave Austin. It would have pleased him a lot more if he'd been sure the attacks on Paige would stop once her work was completed.

Other Rangers would continue to guard her, of course. He knew that. He also knew that nobody was going to keep an eye on her the way he had—with every ounce of his spirit as well as his heart.

EIGHTEEN

The sun had set over an hour ago. Paige's shoulder and neck muscles were screaming at her to stop working. She refused to give in. She also refused to keep looking at the area across the room where the Ranger had made himself at home, his boots propped on her desk like a footstool, his hat once again shading his eyes. He'd been sitting like that for so long she wondered if he was asleep.

The ringing of his cell phone and the slow, deliberate way he sat up demonstrated full control and proved he'd been playing possum.

Although she kept her attention focused on the bust of the crime victim, she managed to listen to Cade's words. He'd wasted so few of them on her during that particular day she was thirsty for the sound of his voice and the way its vibrations made her tingle all the way to the roots of her long, brown hair.

This time, to Paige's relief, Cade didn't sound angry.

"Hi, Dad. What's up?" He got to his feet, cupping the phone and ambling toward the door. "Yeah. I'm still in Austin."

Her hands trembled enough that she laid down the

tool she'd been using to accent the hairs in the clay eyebrows.

"No. I didn't." Cade paused and glanced at her. "No. I don't think so."

Holding very still, Paige remained seated on the tall stool beside her worktable and refused to flinch under his obvious scrutiny.

"It's just not going to work out, Dad," he finally said. "Hold on a sec."

Cade lowered the instrument, covered it with his other hand and spoke directly to her. "I'm going to step into the hall to finish this call. Don't try to sneak out. I'll be right there."

Her jaw slackened. She wanted to insist she was honest and trustworthy but it was evident he was not ready to hear anything like that, let alone accept it as fact.

Nodding, she pressed her lips into a thin line, swiveled the stool and the bust so she'd have a plausible excuse to break eye contact and went back to work.

It wasn't until she heard the door close behind Cade that she turned back to stare after him, unseeing.

Her heart was truly breaking. If this was the answer to those fervent prayers she'd recently prayed, she'd sure hate to see what would happen if she hadn't asked for the Lord's guidance.

Unshed tears gathered behind her lashes. "I'm sorry if I blew it, Father. Really, I am. I was doing my best, the same way I always have. The same way I did when Amy was kidnapped."

Since her hands had clay on them, she swiped at her damp cheeks with the back of her wrist. "I am so, so sorry. Please forgive me."

This time, instead of feeling elation or hope, she was overcome by a sense of peace. It flowed down over her slowly, gently, as if someone were pouring warm oil on her hair and letting it cover her, body and soul.

The tears she'd been holding back followed until she was weeping openly and unashamed, as if they were completing the cleansing her spontaneous prayer had begun.

Cade remained in the hallway, although he did step away from Paige's studio door so there wouldn't be any chance of her overhearing the rest of his conversation.

"Look, Dad. It's just not going to happen."

"She told you she wouldn't come for Thanksgiving?"

"I never asked her. She drives me crazy, okay?"

"How? What does she do that's so bad?"

"She…" Cade searched for the right words. He didn't want to rehash everything that had happened so he simplified. "She *thinks.*"

Sam chortled. "What's wrong with that? At least your kids will be smart."

"There won't be any kids, Dad. At this point I doubt I'll ever get married, so forget it."

"Have it your own way."

Cade could tell that his father was still highly amused. "It's not funny."

"Fine. Care to tell me what put the burr under your saddle? Maybe if you talk about it you'll see how silly it is to throw away a good woman just because she's a little headstrong."

"A little? Paige is the most stubborn, hardheaded person I've ever met, except maybe for you."

"Then she's in good company." Another guffaw sounded smothered, as if Jacob were trying to mute it. "Say, I have an idea. I've been a widower for a long time. How about introducing me to that lady? She sounds like *my* type, even if she's not yours."

"Wash your mouth out you dirty old man," Cade gibed, having to laugh in spite of himself. "Paige is too good for you." He paused then finally said, "You're right. I can't stand thinking of her as any other man's wife."

"Good. So, when're you gonna come to your senses and ask her to dinner? Time's a-wastin'. Thanksgiving's next week."

"I know. And like I said, I'll be in San Antonio and coming home every night by that time." Hesitating, he stood with his back to the outer door and stared at the entrance to the studio where Paige was working so hard.

Heaving a deep sigh, Cade followed it with, "Okay. You win. I'll talk to her about having holiday dinner with us before I leave Austin. Will that satisfy you?"

"Hey, I'm not the one to satisfy. How does it set with you, son?"

"Beats me. She's impossible. I can't trust her to do things my way, even when her life may be in danger."

"Sounds like a normal woman to me," Jacob said. "Talk to you later. Call me back after you've invited her, will you?"

Cade nodded. "Yeah. I promise. Just don't get your hopes up too high. She still may turn me down. We haven't exactly been seeing eye-to-eye lately."

His father was still laughing when they bid each other goodbye. Cade pushed the button on his cell to end the connection and stuffed the phone back into his pocket. What could he possibly say to break the ice with Paige? he wondered. She certainly hadn't been talkative today. Then again, neither had he.

Glancing down the deserted, semidark hallway he thought about stopping in to see Captain Parker the following morning and feeling him out about a possible transfer to the Austin office.

No, Cade decided immediately. If he left Company D it might remove him from the investigation into Captain Pike's murder. He wasn't going to walk away from that. Not now. Not ever.

Deep in thought, he shoved both hands into his jacket pockets and just stood there.

The next thing he knew, his head was exploding with pain and he felt himself losing consciousness.

With his last thought, he threw himself forward and stretched a hand toward the door to Paige's studio. His fingertips brushed the knob.

Paige had fitted a short, brown, man's wig on to her finished sculpture and had used her digital camera to photograph the result from all sides while Cade was gone.

She plugged the camera into her computer and downloaded the new images, then emailed them to all the Ranger divisions before leaning back and closing her eyes.

It was over. Finally. She turned her attention in the direction of the door. What was keeping Cade? His father must have had a lot more to say than that grumpy Ranger had lately.

Should she open the door and tell him she was done?

"Uh-uh. Not after the lecture he gave me when he left," she muttered. "If he wants to see this reconstruction he's just going to have to force himself to come back in and face me."

A subtle sound beyond the door caught her attention. Since everyone else in the office had gone home long ago, she assumed Cade had locked the door on his way out and was fiddling with his key.

"Is that you?" she called, closing the distance. "You could have knocked, you know."

Pressing an ear to the door she tried again. "Cade?"

As she waited, she felt fear begin to nibble at her. Then, the lights went out the same way they had the first night he'd visited her studio and she jumped as if she'd received an electric shock.

"Hey, this isn't funny. You know I don't like the dark!"

Still, the Ranger didn't reply. Could he be testing her to see if she'd follow his instructions to the letter? It was a remote possibility. Very remote, she argued. Cade might be bossy but he wasn't cruel. Paige was certain he'd never purposely try to scare her. Whoever had killed the lights had to be up to their old tricks and still bent on stopping her from identifying the skull. Well, it was too late for that. She'd finished her sculpting and the views of that face were already spread all over Texas. No matter what else happened, she'd done her job.

What had become of Cade? she wondered, so worried she could barely make herself concentrate, let alone spring into decisive action the way she knew he would have.

Her hand closed on the knob. She twisted. As soon as the latch let go, a shadowy object at the base of the door pushed it partway in. There wasn't enough light filtering through the window from the parking lot to tell much, but Paige knew without a doubt that the object crumpled on the floor at her feet was Cade Jarvis.

She crouched and laid a tremulous hand on his head, then pushed her fingers through his thick hair. Although his body was warm, she was certain she'd felt blood pulsing from his scalp. That was a good sign. If he wasn't alive, he wouldn't still be bleeding like that.

Cloaked in a silent darkness that pressed in as if trying to smother her and render her ineffectual, Paige held her ground. She wanted to run, to scream, to hide and cover her head the way she had after she'd run away to go looking for Amy and had wandered the darkened park grounds until the police had finally seen her and made her go home.

No outsiders were going to come to her aid this time. If there was any rescuing to be done, she was going to have to do it. Alone.

And *soon*, she added, gritting her teeth. Grabbing a handful of Cade's jacket, she started to drag him through the door so she could lock it again.

Footfalls, padded but unmistakable, resonated down the empty hallway from her left. And they were getting louder. Someone was running her way. Fast.

Panic gave Paige the added strength she needed. With a mighty yank she jerked Cade the rest of the way, kicked his booted feet out of the opening and slammed the door just as a heavy body crashed against it from the other side.

A curse in Spanish. More muttering. Kicks at the base of the door. In a distant corner of the room Max began to growl, apparently so frightened he'd gone into hiding.

Paige threw the deadbolt and leaned against the door. How long would it hold? What should she do next?

At her feet she heard a soft moan. Forgetting everything else, she dropped to the floor and gently cradled Cade's head in her lap. He stirred and tried to sit up.

"Whoa. Take it easy, cowboy. You've been out cold."

He rubbed his head and winced when his fingers touched the injury. "Somebody must have hit me from behind."

"Guess so."

Managing to raise on one elbow, he peered into the gloom. "Where am I?"

"Back in my office."

"But…how did I get here? The last thing I remember is being in the hall."

"Yeah, well, I disobeyed your orders again and opened the door after all the lights went out." She couldn't see his expression but did feel his muscles knot where her hand was resting on his shoulder. Before he could express more displeasure, she added, "And it's a good thing I did or you'd still be lying out there with the guy who's been trying to break in. Thankfully, the door is holding."

"What guy? Did you see anybody?"

"No." She assisted him as he struggled to regain his equilibrium and stand, although he was still unsteady. "Lean on me."

"Wait," Cade said. "Listen. I don't hear anybody trying to jimmy the door. Do you?"

"Not now. He was a minute ago. He was speaking Spanish, too."

"What did he say?"

"I recognized a few words. They aren't ones I intend to repeat."

"Okay. Get over behind the computer table and stay down."

"What're you planning to do? You can't fight him hand-to-hand when you can hardly balance."

"I'll think of something."

Paige was about to tell him exactly what she thought of his non-plan plan when she heard his quick intake of breath. Her heart leaped into her throat and lodged there. "What's wrong? Are you sick?"

To her surprise and relief, he laughed quietly. "Nope. Just checked my holster. The guy must have thought he'd finished me off because he didn't bother to take my gun. Here." He thrust his cell phone at her. "Call 911."

She immediately complied. "Done. Help is on the way. What else?"

"Nothing. We wait."

To Paige's delight, Cade slipped an arm around her and guided her to the spot where he'd told her to hide. She didn't care where she was as long as he was with her. The addition of his closeness and display of affection, however slight, was merely the icing on the best cake she'd ever eaten. There was nothing like a good scare to bring people together, was there? Especially if they survived.

She cuddled closer. "You figure on thanking me for rescuing you anytime soon?"

"I may." His voice lost its softness. "Hush."

"Why? What…?"

"The window." Releasing her, he raised up enough to rest both hands atop the computer table. They were gripping his .45 and aiming it at the only source of light, the parking lot.

A man-shaped shadow came between them and the outside reflections, then seemed to back away.

Cade tensed.

Paige screamed as a body burst through the glass. The attacker fired wildly, acting bent on killing anything and everything in the room.

Cade's gun jerked once. Flames leaped from the end of the barrel. Everything became deathly still.

Keeping his .45 trained on the place where he'd thought the man had landed, he flicked on his flashlight, then approached and carefully checked the vital signs of the body.

Satisfied that the danger was over for good, he returned and pulled Paige into his arms. She was shaking but not crying the way he'd expected her to.

"You okay?" he asked.

"Yes. You?"

"Fine. That guy was shooting too wildly to hit anything."

"Is he dead?"

"Yes." Cade felt her arms tighten around his waist.

"Positive?"

"No question." He sighed as he stroked her back to help calm her. "It might have been better if we'd been able to question him but I couldn't see well enough to choose my target. I just had to aim for the muzzle flash and hope."

"And pray," Paige added. She was smiling up at him when the lights came back on.

Squinting, Cade gave her a quizzical look, said, "Oh?" and was thrilled to see her nod.

She wrapped her arms around his neck and pulled him closer, leaving absolutely no doubt she was asking to be kissed.

More than happy to oblige, he claimed her lips as if he'd waited all his life for that moment. Paige responded in kind.

Cade wondered how long they would have stood like that if a uniformed Trooper's arrival hadn't interrupted them.

Grinning, he'd squeezed her tight for one last moment, leaned his head back, closed his eyes and thanked God for everything. It was a long, long list. One he hoped to add to for the rest of his life—with Paige.

EPILOGUE

Enjoying Thanksgiving dinner with Cade and his father, Jacob, at their ranch north of San Antonio seemed so natural to Paige she was floored. Both men were going out of their way to make her feel at home and their efforts were succeeding beautifully. Not only was she impressed with the ranch itself, she was also surprised at how easy the drive was from her place on the southern outskirts of Austin.

Cade's small, quaint house was nearly as charming as its occupants, with furnishings that weren't a bit ostentatious. Happily, her own home was also habitable again and daily life had gotten back to normal. Angela had recovered fully and had enrolled in a self-defense class. Cade had acted amused, especially after Paige had informed him that she was going to take the class, too.

Jacob directed a question to his son. "I hear things have settled down in Austin. Who was the guy who crashed through the window and made you shoot him?"

"Rick Martinez," Cade replied. "Like we'd figured, he was another underling working for the Lions of Texas."

"What about that face Paige recreated?"

"It belonged to Axle Hudson, a very wealthy man who had been missing for about two years. He wasn't a criminal so his DNA wasn't on file with CODIS. We got a positive match after his estranged wife provided a sample of his hair."

"That's good. You gonna go check her out?"

"He'd better not," Paige offered with a grin. "Captain Parker says he has to take time off until the doctors are happy with his cracked head."

"There's nothing wrong with me. I keep telling them that but they won't listen."

"I understand the captain is sending Lieutenant Daniel Riley to speak to the widow," Paige said. "He seems quite capable."

Chortling, Jacob nodded. "Probably is. My son thinks there's nobody but him who can handle the tough jobs. It's a family trait."

"So I've heard."

The older man turned and reached for a pie that was waiting on the sideboard. "Who's ready for dessert? How about it, Paige? Do you like pumpkin? I've got whipped cream, too."

"I love pie. Thanks."

"Cade baked it himself." Jacob gave her a sly grin and a wink.

She could tell by the resulting expression on the Ranger's face that his father was stretching the truth past the breaking point. Nevertheless, she played along. "Good. I love a man who can cook."

Jacob chortled. "My Maryanne did, too." Squirting a dollop of whipped cream topping on her pie before passing it to her, he added, "So, when are you two getting married?"

If Paige had had a mouthful right then, she knew she'd have blown dessert all over the table.

Cade wasn't doing much better at hiding his shock. "Dad! Stop it."

Shrugging, Jacob continued to dish up their pie as if he hadn't done a thing wrong. "Well, you did say your kids would be brilliant with Page for a mother, so I figured it was only a matter of time."

She knew her mouth was open almost as wide as her eyes were when she swung her gaze to Cade.

"Dad said that. I didn't."

Biting her lip to keep from bursting out laughing, she watched his complexion go from a light tan to something akin to a boiled lobster before she spoke up. "Oh, really? You don't agree that I'm smart? I could tell you my IQ if you need to be impressed."

"I didn't mean it *that* way."

Paige lost what little self-control she'd had left. Just being there with Cade was so wonderful and perfect, yet so nerve-racking, she'd been on the verge of getting the giggles all afternoon. Seeing him caught off balance like that pushed her emotions over the edge.

In seconds, she was laughing so hard she was doubled over. She covered her face with her napkin. Tears streamed down her cheeks.

Across the table, Sam was in a similar state of hilarity.

When Paige finally caught her breath and looked up, however, Cade was not only not laughing, he had approached and was down on one knee beside her chair.

"If you think the idea of us getting married is really that funny, maybe I shouldn't ask."

It was the tender expression on his face, not his words, that melted her heart and made her reach to caress his cheek. "Be careful, cowboy," she whispered. "I just might say yes."

"Is that a threat or a promise?"

"Definitely a promise," Paige said.

She leaned closer so he could kiss her the way he had after their ordeal had finally ended. This time, they had a retired State Trooper as a witness instead of a current one, but Paige didn't care. After all, Jacob was practically family already.

She pressed her lips to Cade's and sighed. She could hardly wait for the next blessing the good Lord had in store for her. If it was half as good as this one, she knew it would take her breath away.

* * * * *

Dear Reader,

As you have probably already noticed, this is book #3 in the Texas Ranger Justice miniseries. You'll find the other five titles, and the names of their authors, listed in this book. When our publisher asks us to work together to form an ongoing story we always enjoy the challenge, even though it can sometimes be frustrating and confusing.

In *Face of Danger,* Paige Bryant is also confused. Problems in her past have left her wondering whether God even exists, let alone answers her prayers. It isn't until she stops trying to do everything under her own power and turns back to the faith of her childhood that she finally receives the help she seeks. It isn't complicated. All a person has to do is ask God, with an open heart, and He will be there for you as Paige, and I, have learned.

I love to hear from readers. The quickest replies are by email, Val@ValerieHansen.com, or check out my website, www.ValerieHansen.com. By regular mail, you can reach me at PO Box 13, Glencoe, AR 72539.

Blessings,

Valerie Hansen

QUESTIONS FOR DISCUSSION

1. Is there anything in your childhood that might keep you from being happy today? Can you think of it without being sad or angry?

2. Looking back as an adult, do you wish you had handled a childhood situation differently? How? Might you have made things worse instead of better?

3. Is it possible that everything was working for your good, even if you didn't realize it at the time? Look at Paige's life and see where her trauma eventually brought her.

4. Have you ever been afraid of the dark? I am. I have a terrible time controlling my imagination, even though I do trust God. Does that seem sensible? Why or why not?

5. Because Cade is so dedicated to his job and to helping people, was it harder for him to admit he didn't have all the answers? Could pride be his problem?

6. It's easy to be sorry for things we've done in the past. Have you found it hard to forgive *yourself*? Do you think God is like that, or is He able to forgive everything if we simply ask?

7. Cade can be bossy when he feels others need protecting. Is he right to act that way? Is it more in a

man's nature to do so than in a woman's? Does that trait drive you as crazy as it does me? ☺

8. I love dogs, which is probably why Paige is so strongly attached to her sheepdog, Max. In this case, however, might she be using the dog's unquestioning acceptance to soothe her fear that she's fallen short of pleasing people?

9. Is your family cold or distant, the way Paige's parents were after her sister was kidnapped? Is there a reason to try to forgive those who treat you badly?

10. When two headstrong individuals meet, are they likely to fall in love easily or do you think it will be harder for them than for a couple where one is strong-willed and the other more easygoing?

11. We actually began work on this series before there was such an explosion of trouble on the southern borders of Texas. If you lived there, would you change your daily habits or do you think the press is overpublicizing the drug wars?

12. Paige and Angela are basically defenseless when they're home alone. Do you feel the same? Is it possible that God expects us to defend ourselves, at least by using our wits?

13. Paige makes mistakes. More than once. So does Cade, even if he won't admit it. Is it sensible for her, when she knows she's in danger, to listen to her heart instead of her brain?

14. When Paige is in danger and Cade comes to her rescue, why does she imagine him as some kind of superhero? Can a normal person take on a more important role through circumstances? Does that really change who they are?

15. There can be a danger in assuming we know everything important about a person in a very short time. Was Paige foolish to fall in love so fast? If this was real life instead of fiction, do you think she'd have been wiser to wait before agreeing to spend the rest of her life with the Ranger?

*With the mystery skeleton identified as Axle Hudson,
Texas Ranger Daniel Boone Riley—and the bad guys—
think the man's estranged wife, Melora, knows more
than she's letting on. Read on for a preview of
TRAIL OF LIES by Margaret Daley, the next
exciting book in the Texas Ranger Justice series,
available April from Love Inspired Suspense.*

Melora Hudson punched in her alarm code to turn the security system off, then tossed her keys on the counter in her kitchen. All she wanted to do was sink into a chair and drink a cup of hot tea after the exhausting past week. But as she moved toward the kettle on the stove, a sound—something hitting the tiled floor—coming from the living room made her freeze in midstride. Tension whipped through her—until her cat shot through the doorway, racing straight for her and launching himself into her arms.

"Okay, Patches, what have you gotten into this time?"

Melora cuddled the fifteen-pound white cat against her chest and started for the living room. She approached the entrance, mentally preparing herself for what he'd destroyed, realizing she could never get rid of the animal because her daughter loved him.

A few steps into the room, Melora came to an abrupt halt, scanning the large expanse for any sign of what had made the crashing noise.

Finally she saw the overturned desk chair at the far end. Strange. How did Patches do that? She placed the large cat on the tiled floor and started across the room. Nothing he did should surprise her anymore. She began to pick up the chair but stopped. Her nape prickled, streaking unease down her spine. She glanced toward the study.

She wasn't alone.

She whirled around and ran toward the back porch off the great room. Halfway to the exit, she noticed the lock wasn't turned right.

The door was unlocked.

She peered sideways and spied a wiry, medium-size man wearing a black ski mask and barreling toward her. Pushing herself faster, she reached toward the knob.

He tackled her to the floor. The impact with the cool tiles knocked the breath from her. He trapped her beneath him.

She twisted and bucked, trying to shove him off her. She drew in a gulp of oxygen-rich air. Finally her protest ripped from her throat and ricocheted off the tall ceilings, filling every crevice with her terror.

Follow this gripping tale in
TRAIL OF LIES by Margaret Daley,
available April, only from Love Inspired Suspense.

REQUEST YOUR FREE BOOKS!

2 FREE RIVETING INSPIRATIONAL NOVELS
PLUS 2 FREE MYSTERY GIFTS

Love Inspired®
SUSPENSE

YES! Please send me 2 FREE Love Inspired® Suspense novels and my 2 FREE mystery gifts (gifts are worth about $10). After receiving them, if I don't wish to receive any more books, I can return the shipping statement marked "cancel". If I don't cancel, I will receive 4 brand-new novels every month and be billed just $4.24 per book in the U.S. or $4.74 per book in Canada. That's a saving of at least 23% off the cover price. It's quite a bargain! Shipping and handling is just 50¢ per book in the U.S. and 75¢ per book in Canada.* I understand that accepting the 2 free books and gifts places me under no obligation to buy anything. I can always return a shipment and cancel at any time. Even if I never buy another book, the two free books and gifts are mine to keep forever.

123/323 IDN FDCT

Name _____ (PLEASE PRINT) _____

Address _____ Apt. #

City _____ State/Prov. _____ Zip/Postal Code

Signature (if under 18, a parent or guardian must sign)

Mail to the Reader Service:
IN U.S.A.: P.O. Box 1867, Buffalo, NY 14240-1867
IN CANADA: P.O. Box 609, Fort Erie, Ontario L2A 5X3

Not valid for current subscribers to Love Inspired Suspense books.

Are you a subscriber to Love Inspired Suspense
and want to receive the larger-print edition?
Call 1-800-873-8635 or visit www.ReaderService.com.

* Terms and prices subject to change without notice. Prices do not include applicable taxes. Sales tax applicable in N.Y. Canadian residents will be charged applicable taxes. Offer not valid in Quebec. This offer is limited to one order per household. All orders subject to credit approval. Credit or debit balances in a customer's account(s) may be offset by any other outstanding balance owed by or to the customer. Please allow 4 to 6 weeks for delivery. Offer available while quantities last.

Your Privacy—The Reader Service is committed to protecting your privacy. Our Privacy Policy is available online at www.ReaderService.com or upon request from the Reader Service.

We make a portion of our mailing list available to reputable third parties that offer products we believe may interest you. If you prefer that we not exchange your name with third parties, or if you wish to clarify or modify your communication preferences, please visit us at www.ReaderService.com/consumerschoice or write to us at Reader Service Preference Service, P.O. Box 9062, Buffalo, NY 14269. Include your complete name and address.

THE LAST UNNAMED MAGIC SWORD

~~~~~~~~~~~~~~~~~~~~~~~~~~~~~~~~~~~~~~

On the table lay a sword—a great, magnificent sword. Its fancy hilt looked like polished gold, and its blade shone with unbelievable brightness.

"A true magic sword," the sorcerer said. "Forged by the ancient dwarf kings thousands of years ago. It has never been used. It is a virgin sword. You must name it, Joe— name it for all time."

"Uh—name it?"

The sorcerer nodded. "Just take it, hold it in front of you, and give it a name with real meaning. You should feel honored. This may be the last unnamed magic sword in existence."

Joe did as instructed. The sword glowed and hummed softly. He thought for a moment, then brightened. "Okay. I name this sword—Irving."

"WHAT!" Marge screamed. "Irving? That's ridiculous!"

Joe looked puzzled. "But I *like* the name Irving."

By Jack L. Chalker
Published by Ballantine Books:

THE WEB OF THE CHOZEN

AND THE DEVIL WILL DRAG YOU UNDER

A JUNGLE OF STARS

DANCERS IN THE AFTERGLOW

THE SAGA OF THE WELL WORLD
Volume 1: *Midnight at the Well of Souls*
Volume 2: *Exiles at the Well of Souls*
Volume 3: *Quest for the Well of Souls*
Volume 4: *The Return of Nathan Brazil*
Volume 5: *Twilight at the Well of Souls:*
   The Legacy of Nathan Brazil

THE FOUR LORDS OF THE DIAMOND
Book One: *Lilith: A Snake in the Grass*
Book Two: *Cerberus: A Wolf in the Fold*
Book Three: *Charon: A Dragon at the Gate*
Book Four: *Medusa: A Tiger by the Tail*